Making an Impact

Michele Shriver

SMC Publishing

Making an Impact: A Men of the Ice Novella
By Michele Shriver
Copyright 2016 Michele Shriver
Published by SMC Publishing
All Rights Reserved

ISBN-13:
978-1537740867

ISBN-10:
1537740865

"Age is no barrier. It's a limitation you put on your mind." - Jackie Joyner-Kersee

CHAPTER ONE

F orty. There *was* life after forty. Charlene Simmons proved it, because she crossed the milestone at 12:22 p.m. Central Standard Time and was still awake, alive and breathing. That was the good news. The bad news was that she was also single, alone, and at this particular moment in time, depressed.

Perhaps depressed was too strong a word. Char knew people who struggled with chronic depression, and she understood the seriousness of it. Besides, she didn't have an official diagnosis of depression. Char simply wasn't happy about turning forty and being single, so more appropriately, she should perhaps be called a moody old maid, and not depressed.

"Moody old maid. There you go. That's more like it," Char muttered to herself as she eased her brand-spanking-new cherry red Mustang convertible into a parking space in front of the Electric Eel Nightclub. The car had been an early birthday present to herself, and why not? She had the money, and worked hard for it, and since she had no husband and would probably never have kids, why not spend it on herself?

Char worked as the Executive Director of the San Antonio Generals Hockey Club Charity Foundation, a position she considered to be her dream job. Over the past year and a half, since the Generals began their first season of play in the National Hockey League, the Foundation had raised millions of dollars for various charities throughout the San Antonio area. One of the most successful fundraisers to date was the Bachelor Auction to raise money for the awareness and prevention of teenage suicide.

Char used that occasion to arrange a date for her best friend, news anchor Jessica Rowan, with Generals forward Ryder Carrigan. Despite a few rocky moments, their first date blossomed into love, with Ryder and Jess now firmly established as a couple. Char was thrilled for them, because Jess deserved the happiness, but sometimes she still wondered where her happiness was. She sure hadn't found it with Graham, since their marriage had lasted all of three years, and looking back, had probably only been happy for about half of that.

She couldn't quite explain why, since she loved her job and loved her life, but Char's moodiness over not finding her happily ever after had grown more pronounced over the past several weeks, leading up to the big Four-Oh milestone. It was silly to get so worked up over a birthday. Age was only a number after all. That's what everyone said, anyway, but Char still had a hard time accepting said number as her age.

She didn't want to do anything special to mark the birthday, and she sure didn't want to spend it at a night club. She wanted to go home, fix dinner and sit on the couch drinking wine while she watched a sappy movie. Instead, Jess had insisted Char join her at the Electric Eel for a celebratory drink. Fine. One drink, then she could go home and have her pity party, complete with chocolate popcorn.

Char took a minute to smooth her dress when she got out of the car. The little black dress. One she hadn't worn in years, but still managed to fit into thanks to a fairly relentless gym regimen. It was the one saving grace of this day. If she had to turn forty, Char at least wanted to look good for the age.

The club was dark when she pulled open the door, and Char wondered if she had the right place. Why did Jess suggest meeting at a nightclub? If they had to do something to commemorate Char's birthday, why couldn't it just be dinner?

"Surprise!"

Char heard the shouts as the lights turned on, and she found herself facing Jess, Ryder, and a handful of other people from the hockey club, including a few of the players from the team, along with a whole bunch of black balloons and streamers, all proclaiming her new age. Great.

"Are you serious?" Char asked. "You decided to throw me a surprise party?" She didn't know whether to be angry, mortified, or flattered, that's how screwed up her emotions were lately.

"Yes, I did," Jessica said. "And don't even bother yelling at me, because it won't change anything." She held out a crown that said 'Forty and sexy' and said, "Here. Put this on."

"'Forty and sexy?'" Char raised an eyebrow. "I thought it was supposed to be forty and fabulous. Not that that's any better, or more accurate."

"Oh, stop it. Both are accurate. I chose this one." Jessica placed it on Char's head. "Just have fun tonight. No one deserves it more than you."

Happy. She should try for happy. After all, Jess went to a lot of trouble to plan the party. Char could at least attempt to have a good time.

***

Casey Denault's reputation as a playboy and a party animal was well-earned. When it came to women and sex and parties, he seldom said no. Especially not when his attendance at a party was as a favor to one of his teammates. Reputation aside, Casey was all about helping his team.

He only knew Charlene Simmons in passing, having met her at a few of the team's charity events, but Ryder was one of Casey's best friends, as well as his linemate. His wingman, in essence, since Casey played center to Ryder's left wing. That made his decision a no brainer. When Ryder asked a few guys on the team to attend a surprise birthday party for his girl's best friend, who also happened to work for the team, Casey was first in line to accept.

It was weird, being the single guy, since many of his teammates were pairing off now, but here he was, nursing a beer and hanging out in the corner until it was time for the big shout of 'Surprise.' Okay, duty done. How long did he have to stay? Would there be any other guests? Like, say, any other women? Preferably hot, single women who were looking to score?

Casey would get some ribbing from the other guys if they were privy to his thoughts, but fortunately they weren't. Anyway, he did his part by showing up. Now he'd finish his drink and make his exit; go somewhere a little more exciting. Translation: Some place with a lot more single women.

He didn't want to be rude, though, especially as much as Ms. Simmons did for the Generals organization. Besides, she was one very attractive woman, with brunette hair that fell just past her shoulders and green eyes. There was no point in denying it. She might be sixteen years older, but Casey found her damn hot. That silly crown that was perched on her head, proclaiming her to be 'forty and sexy' sure didn't lie. Maybe it was true what some said about women getting better with age. Casey wondered if it was also true about women and their sexual peak. *No. Don't go there.* That was dangerous territory for sure.

Either way, Casey decided to stay at the club a little longer. "Hi, Ms. Simmons," he said, stepping up beside her at the bar. He set his now-empty empty beer bottle down.

"Call me Char," she said. "The other makes me feel old, which is the last thing I need right now." She let out a chuckle, just one, and barely that. Definitely not a full laugh, and it struck Casey as forced. Yeah, this birthday was hard for her. He didn't know why, but he could sense it was.

"Okay, then. Char." He flashed his most dazzling smile. Well, most women found it dazzling, anyway. Would she prove to be the one that was immune? "I'm Casey Denault, but you already know that."

"Yes, I think everyone knows who you are." Another laugh, longer this time, and it seemed to carry a little humor with it, too, even if it was at Casey's expense. He didn't mind. He liked the sound of her laugh, as well as the twinkle that appeared in her green eyes. One that hadn't been there a moment before.

"Ah, my reputation precedes me. You shouldn't believe everything you hear, though." Casey extended his hand. "Would you care to dance with me, birthday girl?"

***

Char hesitated. She knew Casey's reputation, and it wasn't a good one. Not at all. Then again, maybe he had a point that she shouldn't believe everything she heard. Whenever the Foundation asked any of the players to volunteer their time for charitable causes throughout the community, Casey was among the first to step up and offer his time, or anything else that was requested.

She couldn't deny he was good-looking, with sandy brown hair that hung over his forehead, gray-blue eyes, and a boyishly sexy grin. Char didn't doubt that if Casey played on the Generals' top line, rather than being stuck on the depth chart behind the team captain and face of the franchise, Colton Tremblay, he'd be considered one of the most eligible bachelors in the NHL. Instead, he flew somewhat under the radar, as a second-liner on an expansion team, and playing in a non-traditional hockey market. In spite of that, it didn't take him long to earn the title of the team's biggest playboy, especially once Colton shed his bad-boy image, settled down and recently became engaged.

"Come on, what do you say?" Casey grinned as

he reached for her hand. "I don't bite."

He was cocky, for sure, but so damn cute at the same time. What the heck. She'd promised Jess that she'd try to have a good time. Besides, it was only one dance. Char drained her glass of wine and set the empty glass down before taking Casey's hand. "When you put it like that, how can a girl refuse?"

She let him lead her to the dance floor. The DJ was playing *1999*, a song Char liked, so it was easy to settle into a dancing rhythm. Casey's moves weren't fantastic, but they weren't bad, either, and she found herself relaxing. She had been too tense lately, and Jessica obviously sensed it. Maybe thus surprise party wasn't such a bad idea after all. "Thanks for the dance," Char said when the song came to an end all too quickly.

"One more?" Casey asked, his brows arching up.

As tempting as the offer was, Char planned to decline. Casey was cute, yes, but way too young. Besides, he wasn't interested in her. He couldn't possibly be. Then Bryan Adams' *(Everything I do) I do it for You* began to play. One of Char's favorite songs. Jess must have had a hand in this playlist. "I don't know. Are you sure you don't bite?"

"Only if you ask me to." There was that sexy grin again.

"In that case..." There were plenty of reasons to say no, but at the moment, Char didn't care what they were. She settled into his arms for the slow song, which brought back plenty of memories for her. Some were good, others not so much. "This was the most popular song my freshman year of high school."

"Which was?"

"1991."

Casey chuckled. "That's the year before I was born."

Ouch. "Great. Way to make a woman feel even more like an old maid on her birthday." Char planned to have a chat with Jessica about the song selection.

"Sorry," Casey said. "I didn't mean to make you feel bad, or old, or whatever. You're a very attractive woman."

"You mean for an old maid."

"No." Casey shook his head. "I mean you're very attractive, period. That crown you're wearing doesn't lie."

The crown? It took Char a second to realize he meant the silly tiara on her head. Forty and sexy. "You're kidding, right?" He had to be.

"No. I'm dead serious," Casey replied. "Should I kiss you to prove it?"

Char stopped moving to the beat of the music. "What?" He said he was serious, but surely not. Someone must have put him up to this? That had to be it, right? "Am *I* the charity cause now? Kiss the over-the-hill girl to make her feel better on her birthday?"

CHAPTER TWO

Whoa. The accusation made Casey forget about the song for a second. The only thing that mattered was that he said the wrong thing, and he couldn't quite figure out how. He thought he was being nice, paying Char a sincere compliment. Apparently she wasn't good at accepting them, though.

It must be the birthday, Casey decided. She was having a hard time with this birthday milestone. Old maid, over-the-hill, Casey couldn't keep up anymore. He didn't understand why some people, especially women, got so wrapped up in their age. Maybe he just didn't get it because he was young. Or was it because he was a guy? Either way, it seemed silly to him. Everyone got older. Wasn't that the objective? It beat the alternative. That's what his mom always said.

He sure didn't understand why Char was so down about turning forty, because she wore the age well. Damn well. "Charity? Heck no," Casey said. "I already told you, I find you attractive. Why is that so hard for you to understand?"

"Because, I don't know… Long story." Char let out a sigh. "I'd rather not get into it right now."

Right now? Or with him? Either way, it was personal. Fine. Casey wouldn't pry. "Okay," he said with a shrug. "Let's just dance, then."

"Fine," Char said, and they danced in silence through the song's chorus, Casey knew all the words to it, even though he hadn't even been born when it had been released. Maybe it was because the singer, Bryan Adams, was Canadian, too, or because Casey had seen the movie the song was featured in a couple of times.

"I don't mind if you kiss me, though."

The words jolted Casey from his thoughts. Was she serious? Now she wanted him to? He couldn't keep track, but it didn't matter. He didn't even want to try to understand her. Not now. Char's lips, adorned with a light red lipstick, curled in a half-smile that he found quite sexy, and yes, extremely kissable. For a man who took great pleasure in kissing women—their lips, their necks, their breasts and every other part of their body— that almost-smile, combined with the request, was all Casey needed.

He put his hand at the base of her neck, underneath her hair, and tilted her head, brushing his lips over hers. Only once, then he stopped to take a read on the situation. Char's lips were parted, and her green eyes gazed up at him. In Casey's vast experience with women, that usually meant they wanted more. Once, he'd been wrong and taken a knee to the groin, but that was six years ago. Casey's track record was much improved since.

He took the chance, kissing her again, and sure enough, Char's lips stayed parted, allowing Casey's tongue to dance with hers. She knew how to do this, that was for sure, and she tasted good, too. Very good, and it turned Casey on. Then the music stopped, way too abruptly, and so did the kiss, when Char pulled away.

"Thank you, Casey, for the dance," she said. "And the rest, too." Her eyes twinkled. Yeah, she'd liked it, all right.

"Are you interested in another?" Dance, kiss, whatever. He was flexible. And she was...wow. Casey couldn't think of another word to describe her at the moment. Beauty, brains, devoted to raising money to help others, and damn... she could kiss. Yet there was an insecurity and vulnerability about her, too. Yeah. Wow would have to do.

After a moment, she shook her head. "It's tempting, but I better not."

Why? Was she afraid of where things might lead? Too bad, because that's what Casey wanted to find out. He wouldn't push, though. There were other women. Maybe none this intriguing, with this total package, but plenty of others. "Okay," he said, and gave a shrug of his shoulders, trying to appear nonchalant. "I should probably head out, anyway."

"You're leaving?"

Was it his imagination, or did she look disappointed? "Yeah, I never planned to stay long, but I wanted to come by for a little bit. Happy birthday, Char." Casey smiled. "I hope you're not feeling too down about things."

"I'm better now," she said. "Thank you, again."

Casey's eyes followed her as she walked to the bar, enjoying the way her skirt hugged her hips. Forty and sexy? Make that forty and smoking hot.

***

The kiss left Char breathless and wanting more, but her brain overruled, and she broke it off. She couldn't resist stealing one more glance at Casey, though, before sidling up to the bar. He may be young, basically a kid, but he knew how to kiss. Then again, he got plenty of practice. All the more reason for Char to stay away.

"What'll it be, birthday girl?" the bartender asked.

Char pondered the question. Wine was usually her poison, but a girl only turned forty once. "Give me a strawberry cheesecake martini," she said, and sat down on a barstool. She'd never tried one before, but heard they tasted exactly like the dessert. A claim she didn't entire believe, but left her curious nonetheless.

"You're drinking hard liquor?" The question came from Jessica, and Char tried to read the look on her friend's face. Surprise? Concern? Disapproval? No, not that, but there seemed to be a mix of the first two, at least.

"You told me to have a good time, remember?" The bartender set the martini glass in front of Char, and she picked it up and took a drink. "Well, I'll be damned. It does take like strawberry cheesecake." She held the glass out to Jessica. "Want to try a sip?"

Jessica shook her head. "No thanks."

Char shrugged. "Suit yourself."

Jessica sat down beside her. "Are you okay, Char?" The surprise disappeared, leaving only concern in Jessica's voice.

"I'm fine. Why do you ask?"

"I don't know… because you seem to be taking this birthday even harder than I expected," Jessica said. "I saw you dancing with Casey. *Kissing* Casey. Now you're drinking a martini, which, to my recollection, is a first in the entire ten years I've known you."

Yep. She was concerned, all right. Char didn't blame Jessica. Had the situation been reversed, she'd probably react the same way. "One martini," Char said. "One dance. One kiss." Technically, it had been two dances and two kisses, but the first dance was fast and the first kiss was chaste, so she didn't count those two.

"Yes, but Casey?" Jessica frowned. "Do you think that's a good idea?"

"Casey's not a bad guy." A few minutes ago, she'd been been wary of dancing with him, and here she was defending him. Funny what one kiss could do. "Like I said, it was just a dance and a kiss. Hardly a big deal." Char looked around the club and didn't see him. "He's gone now, anyway." Probably in search of his latest conquest.

"Okay." Jessica sighed. "Sorry. I know you can take care of yourself, but I love you, you know?"

"And I love you, too," Char said. "Look, I am having a hard time with this birthday. It's impacted me more than I thought, and I don't know why. I'll be fine, though. I promise. I'll be back to my old self tomorrow."

"If you say so."

"Yeah, it's just something I need to get over. Thanks for the party. I do appreciate it."

"You're not mad about it, then?"

"Never." Char laughed. "How could I be, when I got this tiara?"

"I thought it was a nice touch." Jessica stood up. "If you're sure you're fine, I'm going to go find Ryder." She nodded in the direction of Char's martini glass. "Take it easy on those, though."

"Don't worry. I'm only having one."

Jessica headed back to the dance floor, and Char finished the drink. True to her word, she declined when the bartender asked if she wanted another. Instead, she got up to leave. The party had been a nice gesture, but she didn't feel like staying.

Outside, Char fished in her purse for her car keys. When she finally found them, she pressed the button to unlock the Mustang, but suddenly felt unsteady on her feet. Maybe that martini wasn't such a good idea. She put her hand on the door to steady herself.

"Char? Is something wrong?"

At the familiar voice, she turned around, to see Casey stepping out of the shadows. "Oh. Casey. I thought you left."

"I was going to, but I didn't get very far, obviously." He whistles as he approached the car. "Sweet set of wheels. Is this yours?"

"Yes. My birthday present to myself. My midlife crisis car, if you will."

"Very nice." He nodded his approval.

"Thanks. I'd offer to give you a spin in it, but that wouldn't be a good idea at the moment." Char put her keys back in her purse. After the brief unsteadiness, she felt better now, but wouldn't chance anything. She had a high profile job she'd prefer to keep, not end up in the police blotter or wrapped around a tree. "I think that martini I had was a mistake on an empty stomach.

Do you want to walk with me to find something to eat?" She didn't know why she asked, other than it wasn't the greatest of neighborhoods to be walking around alone at night. Besides, playboy reputation aside, she'd always known Casey to be a good guy.

"I have a better idea," he said. "I've got a car, and a driver. He can take us anywhere we want to go, if that interests you." Before Char could answer, Casey's lips were on hers again, in a continuation of the kiss inside the club. Make that a continuation with a lot more intensity. When he finally broke off the kiss, she struggled to catch her breath.

"Yes," Char said once she'd found her voice. "That sounds like a great idea."

CHAPTER THREE

S he could use the alcohol as an excuse, but it would be just that—an excuse, and not a very good one. Char didn't feel sober enough to risk driving, but she was in full control of her thoughts and her actions. No, she wasn't getting into the back of a limo with a man sixteen years her junior because she was drunk and uninhibited. She was doing it because she wanted to, plain and simple. Char could own that fact. Maybe it was the best part of turning forty. With maturity came accountability. Or something like that.

"Home, Mr. Denault?" the driver asked, and Casey glanced at Char, his eyes searching hers for an answer.

One more chance to say no. "Sounds good to me."

Casey grinned. "Yes, home it is, Jack, and I don't mind if you take your time getting there." He gave the man a wink which made clear to Char that this wasn't the first time he'd done this. Maybe that should raise a red flag. Maybe she should care. She didn't. There was that accountability thing again.

Casey helped her into the back of the car, and as soon as the privacy screen closed, separating them from the driver, he pulled her onto his lap. Char felt the bulge of his erection through his jeans, and wondered if all he had in mind was a 'quick wham-bam-thank you, ma'am' sort of encounter. It would fit with his reputation, after all. Love 'em and leave 'em. Instead of reaching for his zipper, though, Casey's hand moved between Char's legs, causing a tremor to course through her.

One touch, and he hadn't even gotten close to her pleasure point, and she was shaking. Yes. She needed this. It had been too damn long.

"Are you wet?" Casey asked.

She'd been wet since the kiss inside the club, but wasn't ready to admit it. Instead, she said, "Why don't you touch me and find out?"

"I like the way you think," Casey said, as his fingers found her panties, and her secret was out. "Oh yeah. Nice and wet." He massaged her through the damp fabric.

Char's breath hitched. "That feels good. Don't stop." At the rate this was going, she wouldn't last long.

"Oh, baby, I'm just getting started." Casey pushed aside her underwear with his fingers, then inserted one inside her. "So slick, just the way I like it." He thrust another finger into her. "I bet you taste good, too. I want to taste you, but we'll get to that later…"

Char hoped it was a promise. Either way, Casey had more in mind than a little quickie. No, it was clear he wanted to pleasure her exactly the way she needed, and satisfy her before himself. Char arched her back, grinding against his hips as his fingers worked away inside her. She was close now, so close, and clenched her teeth from crying out, which only made him increase his movements.

"That's it. Come on, baby. I'm going to make you come, and I want you to scream."

Char bit her lip. The first part was a foregone conclusion, and thankfully so, but she remained determined not to scream. The limo driver no doubt knew exactly what was happening in the backseat, but that didn't mean she had to broadcast her climax for him to hear.

Her resolve lasted until Casey's thumb found her clit, and as he massaged it, she couldn't hold out any longer, and couldn't stop herself from screaming, "Oh, God, Casey. Yes!" as her body shook.

The intensity of the climax surprised her, and thankfully, Casey kept his free hand on Char's back, preventing her from knocking her head against the seat behind her, or the privacy screen. "There you go," he said, extracting his fingers from her once her spasms stopped and her breathing slowed. "You're even sexier when you come."

Char didn't quite trust her voice yet, so she only nodded. The limo pulled to a stop, and Casey smiled.

"Perfect timing. We're here."

The timing *was* perfect, too perfect not to be planned, and Char wondered if the driver had simply been going around in circles until he'd heard her cries from the backseat. She moved off of Casey and adjusted her dress just as the door opened.

"Here we are, Mr. Denault." The driver's

expression remained stoic, the face of professionalism and discretion.

"Thank you, Jack," Casey said.

Char surveyed the surroundings and realized they were in front of the Grand Hyatt. "This is where you live? The hotel?"

Casey laughed. "No. I live in one of the luxury condos above the hotel. Room service is one of the perks, so I'll get you that food you need. A little later, though," he added with a wink. "After we finish what we started."

***

Casey was grateful for the private entry to the residence unit atop the hotel, and for no one in the elevator. It took every ounce of willpower and restraint he could muster not to stop the elevator and take her right then and there. His cock throbbed, needing to be free of the confines of his pants, and inside her. Christ, she was incredible.

They got to his unit, and Casey hastily unlocked the door using one hand, while the other tugged at his zipper. The bedroom. He should probably take her to the bedroom, except he didn't think he could wait. No. Later, he would make love to her the right way. Slow and tender. Right now, he just needed to have her, especially when she was already wet and ready for him.

Casey closed the door and backed her against it. "Right here okay? Any objection?" He was losing romance points fast, but hoped to be able to earn them back. Later.

Char gave a shake of her head. "Here's fine, and

hurry, please."

God Bless her. She'd already come, once, and she still wanted him to hurry. Casey choked back a laugh as he pulled a condom from his back pocket. "I don't have any choice in that, baby. You're killing me." He yanked open the rubber and sheathed himself while Char helped the process along by removing her underwear and hiking up her skirt. It afforded Casey the opportunity to see more of her body than he had before, and he liked what he saw.

He longed to explore every inch of her, both with his hands and his mouth. At the moment, though, Casey had a more urgent need. One that couldn't wait. He entered her with ease, her opening already slick and ready for him, and as Char arched her back, Casey thrust deeper.

"More. Faster," she urged, and he held onto her hips as she wrapped her legs around him, and pumped harder.

Casey wanted Char to come first, wanted to see the look of passion in her eyes again as she screamed his name and her whole body shook, and he sensed she was close. He could hold back. He had to. Just a little longer.

He couldn't.

Damn it! Casey cursed himself as he exploded inside her. *Damn it all to hell.* Now she probably thought he was some horny kid who couldn't wait to get his rocks off. Not ready for the big leagues with a woman of her class and sophistication. Pathetic.

As disappointed as he was in himself, Casey didn't want Char to not get her pleasure, so he stayed inside her while he used his thumb on her clit to bring her to climax again. It worked, and it was beautiful to watch, but he still as if he'd let her down. "I'm sorry," Casey said as he pulled out. "I couldn't hold out any longer." He hoped to get the chance to make it up to her.

"Don't apologize, Casey. You've made me feel better tonight that I have in a very, very long time." She kissed him on the lips. "Is there some place I can go freshen up while you order that food you promised me?"

Char's words sealed the deal. She might be the most exquisite woman Casey had ever known, and he didn't want this night to end. And next time, he'd get it right. "Sure. The guest bathroom is down that hall, to the right." He pointed. "First door. There's towels, and a robe, if you want it. Whatever you need. I'll see about getting something to eat brought up."

***

Swanky was the first word that came to mind as Char walked down the hall. She knew there were luxury condos on top of the Grand Hyatt, but she'd never seen them until now. Very swanky. She closed the bathroom door and looked in the mirror. Yes, she'd been rode hard, that was for sure. Her hair was a disheveled mess, her dress wrinkled, and her makeup smudged. Damned if she didn't look satisfied, though. The classic JBF look. Just been fucked. And what a fuck it was. Poor Casey, feeling bad about finishing before her, but still taking the time to get her off with his hands. He had very talented hands, with or without a hockey stick in them.

A fluffy robe adorned with the hotel logo hung from a hook on the door, so Char opted to take a quick shower. She needed it. Afterward, she wrapped herself in the robe and went to find Casey. He stood in the living room, wearing baggy shorts and a Generals T-shirt. His hair was damp, so he must have showered, too.

"Hey," he said. "I wasn't sure what you wanted, so I just ordered a couple club sandwiches and chips. I hope that's okay. If you're vegan, or gluten free, or whatever, I can call them back and get you something else."

Char shook her said. "No, that sounds great. I eat just about anything." And at the moment, she was starving. She frowned as she saw what he held in his hand. "Is that my phone?"

"Oh, yeah, sorry." He held it out to her. "I promise I didn't look at your email or your contacts or anything, but I heard it buzz, so I grabbed it from your bag. You got a call or text or something."

"Thanks." She took it from him. He couldn't snoop at it. She had a passcode on it. Char keyed in the code to unlock the phone and went to her missed calls. She already knew who they were from before she saw Jessica's name. Shit! She'd left her car the club, and now Jessica was paranoid. Char didn't listen to the voice mail, just went straight to her text messages.

Where the hell are you? Your car's still in the lot. Worried. Please tell me nothing happened to you.

Well, something happened, all right, but it was all good. Char made the quick decision not to call Jessica back, knowing it would only bring questions. Instead, she typed a quick reply to the text.

I'm fine. Felt kind of tipsy after that stupid martini, so got a driver to take me home.

It wasn't a lie, except for maybe the last part. She hadn't gone to her home. Char hit send, then followed up:

Just going to bed. I'll call you in the morning after I pick up my car. Sorry to worry you.

She hit send again, then set the phone on the coffee table.

"Everything okay?" Casey asked.

Char nodded. "Yeah, I just scared Jess to death by leaving my car at the club and not saying goodbye." She rolled her eyes. "She worries too much."

"Understandable. There's a lot of sick people in the world," Casey said. "That's why I wasn't going to let you walk anywhere by yourself. Not after dark in a sketchy neighborhood."

It was a good thing Casey had still been outside the club, or she might have walked once she realized she shouldn't drive, even though she should know better. Char wondered if he'd hung around on purpose, hoping she might leave and he'd run into her again. It didn't matter. She was just glad he had hung around, whatever his reason. "Thanks for taking care of me, Casey." Too late, Char realized the double entendre. "Bad choice of words."

"I think it was an excellent choice of words." A knock sounded at the door. "That's the food," Casey said. "Let's eat, then I'll take care of you again."

His wink and suggestive smile made Char blush. "In that case, I'll be sure to eat fast."

MICHELE SHRIVER

CHAPTER FOUR

Char woke before dawn, while Casey still slept. She didn't want to leave his bed, but she couldn't stay. Instead, she got up quietly and put on her black dress from the night before. Not the best attire for six a.m. Great. She made it to forty without ever having to do a walk of shame, but apparently there was a first time for everything. It couldn't be avoided. She couldn't go pick up her car wearing a robe from the hotel.

After she dressed, Char jotted a quick note for Casey. *Thank you for a night I'll never forget. Good luck in the game tonight.* She hoped it was an appropriate thing to say. She didn't have a lot of prior experience with the whole one night stand thing. It seemed rude to leave without so much as a note, especially after what he'd done for her.

Her wardrobe garnered a strange look from the hired driver, but fortunately no snide remarks, and within fifteen minutes, Char was back at the Electric Eel to retrieve her Mustang. She went to her house to change clothes, then called Jessica. No doubt her friend would have a ton of questions. Char couldn't put this off, and she'd made up her mind that she wouldn't lie, either.

"I just got my car," she said when Jess answered. "Do you want to meet somewhere for breakfast?"

"I'd love to. I want an explanation for why you disappeared last night without even saying goodbye."

Yeah, you'll get your explanation. And hopefully you'll understand. "The waffle house on Marshall street?" Char suggested, then ended the call once Jess agreed.

Jess was already seated in a booth when Char arrived at the restaurant. She slid into the opposite side of the booth and raised her hand to flag down a server. "Coffee, and the stronger the better," she said. "Cream and sugar, too, please."

"Are you still feeling the effects of that martini?" Jessica asked, frowning.

Char shook her head. "No. I just didn't sleep very well." Who had time to sleep? "I'm trying to wake up a little before I go into work."

"And you're sure you're okay?"

"Fine," Char insisted. A mug of hot coffee was set in front of her, along with creamer. She added it to the coffee, took a sip, and added more. Her ex-husband always teased her that she added so much cream, she may as well be drinking milk, but Char liked her coffee the way she liked it, and didn't intend to apologize. She also wouldn't apologize for the way she'd spent the night.

"There's something I have to tell you about last night," Char said, "and I ask that you please don't judge me."

"When have I ever judged you?" Jessica looked offended.

"You haven't." *And I hope this isn't about to be the first time.* Char took a drink of coffee, then set the mug down, her hands wrapped around it. "I didn't leave the club alone last night," she said. "I left with Casey."

"What?" As if realizing she all but shouted, Jessica took a look around, then lowered her voice. "Casey? Seriously? Casey?"

"What's wrong with Casey?" Char asked, a touch of annoyance settling in. "And what happened to not judging?"

"I'm not." Jessica held a hand up. "This is me, not judging," she said. "I'm just trying to take this all in. You and Casey? Why on earth would you do that?"

"Because he wanted me, and I wanted him."

"Really? That's it? That's your reason?"

"Yes." Char had no better explanation. That was really it in its purest form. They wanted each other.

"Well... I don't even know what to say, Char. It's hard to wrap my head around this." Jessica paused, drinking from her own mug, and Char sensed she was still struggling with the revelation. "I never thought you were the one night stand type."

"I'm not, or at least I wasn't, and I don't think I will be again," Char said. "I just... needed something, and Casey was able to provide it." She took another drink, looking around the restaurant to make sure their conversation wasn't attracting any onlookers. They didn't have an audience, but Char leaned forward just in case, keeping her voice barely above a whisper. "I had more orgasms last night that I've had in the past year."

Jessica's eyes widened a little. "Okay," she

said. "Which is how many, exactly?"

Char smiled. That's why she considered Jess her best friend. Nope, she wasn't judging. But she *did* want all the juicy details. "Four," she said. "Four. Can you believe that?"

"Whoa. I think maybe I need to talk to Ryder, see if he can top that."

"Don't you dare," Char admonished. "Not a word, to anyone. Least of all, Ryder." She wondered if it would get back to him, anyway. Was Casey the type to brag of his conquests to his teammates? She hoped not, considering the reputation she had to uphold.

"Relax, I'm kidding," Jessica said. "But... wow. You, Casey, four times... It's a lot to absorb. So, um, what happens now? What are you doing to do?"

"Nothing." Char's answer was swift. "I'm going to go to work. Casey will play hockey. We don't have to talk about it again, and it's never going to happen ever again. If I see him, it will strictly be for Foundation business."

"Just like that?" Jessica sounded dubious. "Do you really think you'll be able to do that? Or that Casey will?"

"Oh, I'm sure Casey will have no problem forgetting last night," Char said. "I doubt he'll ever think about me again." The harder question was whether she'd be able to put him out of her mind.

***

Casey was no stranger to the morning after. Usually, it was a relief to wake up and discover that the woman he'd spent the night with had already left. It spared him the awkwardness as he tried to find a way to let them down gently. 'I like you well enough. Last night was great, but I don't do repeat engagements.' Or something like that. Casey always tried to be nice and respectful, but the important thing was that they left, and never bothered him again. Most of the time, it worked. Sure, a few sometimes tried to score another night with him, but Casey had been fortunate that none of them ever turned into crazy stalkers, and they usually got the hint.

Some of his teammates warned Casey his lifestyle would someday get him into trouble, but he prided himself on always being careful. So what if he was the self-proclaimed king of one night stands. He was way too young to restrict himself to only one woman, especially with so many willing women in the world.

So why was he disappointed to wake up to find that Char was already gone, and that she'd left him with only a note thanking him for a wonderful night? That was it. Just a note, and it sounded way too final.

What the hell? Surely he wasn't falling. No way, no how. Casey didn't do that, and not after only one night. Even if it was one incredible night. So incredible, in fact, Casey was still thinking about Char while he was in the shower. The way she'd wrapped her legs around him; the way she'd screamed his name in the throes of passion. And the look in her eyes when she climaxed. No matter what, Casey knew he would never forget that look. The hell with forgetting it. He wanted to see it again. Yeah, he was officially in trouble, and it wasn't the kind of trouble Casey's teammates expected him to get into.

He arrived early to the rink for the team's morning skate, knowing if he were so much as a minute late, he'd be scratched for the game and forced to watch from the press box while he ate nachos. Casey had spent one game, early in his first season with the Generals in the 'Nacho box' after being late for practice, and he'd learned his lesson. It would never happen again. He couldn't help his team win if he wasn't even on the ice.

As early as he was, Casey was still beat by a few players. Their team captain, Colton Tremblay, and alternate captain, Ryder Carrigan, were there and already dressed in their hockey gear. Ryder, whom Casey once dismissed as a stick in the mud. He'd at least learned how to relax a little bit, ever since he started dating the news anchor.

"Hey, Case," Ryder greeted him. "Ready for the game tonight?"

"I think so. Hope so. We have to get these guys this time." The team was scheduled to face the Flyers on the back end of a home and home series, after losing the game played in Philadelphia. The loss left San Antonio six points out of the last playoff spot, and even with more than half the season remaining, every game was important. They couldn't afford to fall further behind.

"We will," Ryder said with confidence. He reached for his gloves. "You didn't stay very long at Char's party last night."

"Nah." Casey tried for a nonchalant shrug. "I had things to do." *Like the birthday girl herself.*

Ryder nodded. "Figured as much. It was nice of you to come by, though. I know Jess appreciated it. She really wanted to make the birthday special for Char."

"Then I hope it was," Casey said. He was pretty sure it had been, and he played a role in that, and not just because he'd shown up at the party. "Happy to do my part."

Casey sat down to lace up his skates. "Now I need to do my part to help this team win." And after the game was over, he'd move on to the next girl, and prove to himself that last night changed nothing. Char hadn't gotten under his skin.

CHAPTER FIVE

C asey loved game nights. He got such a rush of adrenaline at the start of a hockey game, especially the ones at home, where the team had the enthusiasm of their die-hard fans behind them. Coming off of a road trip, the hometown fans were excited to see their team again, and Casey hoped the energy and excitement would help carry them through to a victory. When he scored only a few minutes into the game, Casey sensed he was feeling it, and it was going to be a good night.

As he skated toward the Generals' bench for the customary fistbump with his teammates, Casey's eyes darted to the area a few rows behind the home team bench, where the Generals player's wives and girlfriends usually sat watching them play. It usually didn't bother him that there was no one in the arena rooting specifically for him, but tonight, for some reason, as he took his seat on the bench after the line change, he wondered what it would be like to have someone here for him. Sure, there were plenty of fans in the arena who wore team jerseys with his name and number, but it wasn't the same. They weren't really here for him.

"San Antonio goal scored by number nineteen, Casey Denault, his tenth of the season. Assisted by number fourteen, Ryder Carrigan and number forty-seven, Noah Mann," the Generals in-game arena host announced. "Denault, from Carrigan and Mann. Time of the goal 16:42."

It never, ever got old hearing that, and it gave Casey a further burst of adrenaline. He finished the game with two goals, including the winner late in the third period, giving the Generals a 3-2 victory over the Flyers.

In the locker room afterward , the team mood was jubilant. There was work to do to get back into playoff position, but also time to do it, everyone one in the room understood that. They'd get back to it the next day, but were allowed the night to celebrate the victory, and celebrate was what Casey intended to do.

In keeping with the team's custom, he was awarded the toy gun holster for being the outstanding player of the game. It wasn't the first time Casey had received the honor, but for some reason, this one was special. He put it on to cheers from the rest of the guys.

"Way to go, Case. Good game," Colton praised.

"Thanks, man. I felt good out there tonight. I hope it means I've found my shot again." Casey held his phone up, taking a selfie of himself wearing the holster, and posted it to his Instagram account.

"That's a good look for you," Noah said. "Are you going to leave it on when you go out on the town tonight?"

"I don't know." Casey grinned. "Do you think the chicks will dig it?"

"Maybe. Not that you need any help in that department." Ryder gave a good-natured roll of his eyes.

"Nope, and I doubt tonight will be any exception." Casey preened in the front of the mirror, running a comb through his damp hair. No, he didn't expect to have any trouble finding a willing woman, and that was high on the night's agenda. For all of the cautionary tales that he'd someday get in trouble, or that this lifestyle would eventually grow old, so far it hadn't, so Casey's post-game agenda would be the same as it always after almost every victory. Find a woman and get laid.

***

Char watched the Generals game as she usually did, at home, on her big screen. If the Foundation were hosting a fundraiser, she'd be there in person, such as the next game, when the Founfadtion, along with the player's significant others, would host the second annual holiday toy drive to benefit families in need. Most nights, though, she watched from home, dressed in black leggings and a Generals jersey. Hers had no players name or number customized on the back, because Char had no allegiances other than to the team.

Tonight, though, it was difficult to watch and not get excited about Casey's play. He definitely had his scoring touch out there on the ice. *He sure had it last night in the bedroom, too*, Char thought, followed by, *No. Don't go there. Don't think about him.*

As if that were possible. Char may not want to think about Casey, but putting him out of her mind was proving very difficult, which worried her. It was a one-night stand. It should be easy to forget. Still, she had no regrets about the night. There was some embarrassment, yes, about the lack of restraint and how easily she'd surrendered control. But regret? Definitely not. How could she possibly regret something that felt so damn good?

Char's phone rang as she watched the post-game commentary. She reached for it anxiously, wondering if it might be Casey, which was silly considering he didn't even know her phone number. Instead, it was Jessica, who'd finished up the ten o'clock newscast, which she anchored for channel twelve. "I heard the score. Sounds like your boy toy played a heck of a game tonight," Jessica teased as soon as Char answered.

"My boy toy?" Char rolled her eyes. "Right. Wishful thinking on that."

"What? Now you're saying you *want* him to be your boy toy?" There was no mistaking the amusement in Jessica's tone. Yeah, she was enjoying this.

"That's not what I said. Or what I meant." Or was it, in some Freudian slip sort of way? "You're right about one thing, though. Casey did play a great game. And your guy had a nice assist on the first goal."

"Did he?" Jessica asked. "Great. Hopefully that means Ryder will be in a good mood."

"Are you heading out to meet him now?"

"Yeah, we're going to grab a late night dinner somewhere," Jessica said. "Do you want me to see if he can persuade Casey to come along, and you can join us, too?"

Char couldn't tell if Jessica was serious or not,

but it didn't matter. No way was she accepting that offer. "No," Char said. "I'm going to go to bed. I doubt Casey is the double date type." Or the dating type at all. And she'd just made herself another notch on his bedpost. *Good move, Char. Way to be a mature, classy, respectable woman. Or not.*

"Probably not," Jessica agreed. "Char?"

"Hmm?"

"You're not beating yourself up over last night, are you?"

Oh, how well Jessica knew her. "Maybe a little bit," she admitted. "It's so unlike me."

"Yes, it is, and that's probably why you enjoyed it so much. Don't be too hard on yourself. We've all done things that are out of character. Besides, you're single. You're allowed to have fun. Just not too much, okay?" Jessica teased.

Char laughed. "Don't worry. I'm already back to being my usual boring self." Not even ten thirty and she was on her way to bed. Now, if only she could sleep without thinking about Casey.

***

Casey knocked back a beer before hitting the dance floor with the blonde who'd been eyeing him at the bar. She wasn't a natural blonde—he could tell that from her dark roots—but she had legs that didn't quit and ample breasts that he longed to get a taste of. And from the looks of things, he wouldn't have to work very hard to get that taste. She said her name was Wynter—with a Y—and she was the aggressive type. Most of the time, that didn't bother Casey at all. Easy wasn't a bad quality in a woman. Less work for him, and things tended to happen faster. When Wynter kissed him, though, he tasted cigarettes and whiskey, and the combination wasn't appealing. Instead, it seemed cheap to Casey. And *too* easy.

Casey didn't want cheap. No, he wanted Char. *Damn it all to hell.* She was under his skin, and Casey knew what that meant. Wynter wouldn't do, and neither would any other woman in the bar.

"Can we go back to your place?" Wynter asked. "You have a car waiting, right?"

"What makes you think that?"

"Words gets around." She leaned in closer, her breath hot against Casey's neck. "I hear you always have a driver ready to take your girl of the night back to your house."

His girl of the night? Jesus. Was that what they said about him? Yeah, word got around, and not in a good way. "Sometimes," Casey admitted. "Not tonight, though." He pulled away from her groping hands before his cock got any ideas of its own and decided to respond, because once the blood rushed down there, it would be difficult to say no. "I have to go. It was nice meeting you." Now he was trying to let them down gently *before* he took them home and bedded them, and not the morning after. Did he have Char to thank for that?

Free from Wynter's grasp, Casey went outside and called for his driver. Jack arrived a few minutes later, and gave Casey a puzzled look. "You're alone?"

Was it really so shocking? Evidently so. "Yes, I'm alone," Casey said, getting into the back of the car. "I'm not in the mood for cheap sex tonight."

Was it his imagination, or did Jack smile. "Maybe you're growing up, or you found one that you're falling for, and you don't want to be a disappointment to her."

Yeah. Maybe. "Those your words of wisdom for the night, Jack?"

"Yep. Pretty much all I got."

"Good," Casey muttered. "Then be quiet and drive. I'm anxious to get home."

A smirk appeared in the rear-view mirror. "Yes, boss. Whatever you say."

CHAPTER SIX

C har sat in her office at Generals team headquarters, poring over reports and numbers. It looked like it would be a very good year for the Foundation. The bachelor auction had been a big success. Even better, the cookbook, featuring the players' favorite recipes, brought in a lot of proceeds, all of which would all go to local charities to help combat hunger. The Foundation would end the year with the Second Annual Toy Drive to benefit the local food bank. Char was in the process of emailing her assistant to go over the plans for it when the phone extension on her desk rang. She reached for it without taking her eyes off her computer screen. "This is Char."

"You sound both casual and professional at the same time," a male voice said. "I like it."

Char furrowed her brow as she tried to place the voice, which was oddly familiar. No, it couldn't be. "Casey?"

"You got it on the first try. I'm flattered," he said. "Also curious. Does anyone ever call you by your full first name?"

"Charlene? No. Not once they know me, if they want to live."

A chuckle came over the line. "You don't like it, then?"

"Not really. It's too old-fashioned," she said. "And the last thing I need at the moment is to feel even older than I am."

"Still being hard on yourself, I see."

Was she? Char didn't see it that way. "Actually, I'm having a pretty good day." She chewed on the end of her pen, a nervous habit she wanted to break. It beat smoking, though. She'd kicked that habit ten years ago and didn't plan on picking it up again. "How'd you get my direct line?"

"We have the same employer," Casey said. "I had to be resourceful, since you didn't even leave me your cell number in the note you left by my bed."

"No, I didn't. I figured it was for the best."

"Out of sight, out of mind?"

"Something like that." *Except I can't stop thinking about you.*

"Nice try, in theory," Casey said, "but you're not out of my mind, Char. Not by a long shot."

"Oh." So much for that. Char reached for the can of diet soda on her desk and took a drink. "Why are you calling, Casey?"

"I thought it was obvious. I've been thinking about you. About the other night," he said. "Did you see the game yesterday?"

"Yes. I watched it on TV. You played very well."

"Thanks," Casey said. "I wish you would've been there in person."

Why? What was he getting at? "So do I, given how it turned out," Char said. "I don't go to all the games, but I'll be there for the next few, because we're doing the toy drive again."

"Good," Casey said. "Any chance you'll be wearing my jersey at those games?"

Char frowned. "What?"

"My jersey. You know..."

She did know. The toy drive was co-sponsored by the wives and girlfriends of the Generals players. Last year, Colton Tremblay's fiancée had made her official debut as his girlfriend at the toy drive by sporting his jersey. The team owner's daughter, Meryl Johnson, had similarly made her interest in Russian superstar Nikolai Brantov known by donning his jersey for the event. "You want me to wear your jersey for the toy drive?"

"Well, I want to see you again, that's for darn sure," Casey said. "We'll start there."

Char chewed on the pen again. "I thought you didn't do that. See the women again after you've slept with them." Wasn't he Mr. One and Done?

"I usually don't," Casey replied. "I'll make an exception for you, though. Like I said, you've been on my mind. I thought we had a good connection the other night. Do you really want to end it with just a note? Nothing else? Never knowing where it could lead?"

"No, but—," The words were out before Char could reconsider them.

"Perfect, then," Casey interrupted. "Meet me for lunch. How about Luigi's on Main?"

Char thought about Casey's baked spaghetti recipe that he'd contributed to the cookbook. She hadn't tried it, yet, but it sounded good. "You love your Italian food, don't you?"

"Yep. Always have. I probably should've been Italian instead of French-Canadian," he said. "So what do you say? Do we have a date? At least for lunch?"

She couldn't exactly turn down lunch, could she? After all, she had to eat. Yep. That was her story and she was sticking to it. "Yes, Casey. I'll meet you for lunch, but I can't promise anything more right now."

"That's okay. I'll take what I can get."

***

Luigi's was a casual Italian restaurant that Casey loved for getting his carb fix on game days. This wasn't a game day, but he still craved some good pasta. He was already seated when Char arrived, and he waved her over to his table.

Damn, she's hot, he thought as she headed his way. She wore black jeans that fit perfectly, paired with calf-length leather boots and a gray button-down shirt featuring the Generals team logo on the left side. The same boring shirt that everyone else in the organization wore, and it never got him turned on before, but somehow Char wore it much better. "Unbelievable. You even make that shirt look sexy," he said.

"You flatter me," Char said, pulling out a chair before Casey could do it for her. "I think you're lying, though."

Casey shook his head. "I don't lie to women. I'm guilty of a lot of things, but not that."

"No. You just hope they're already gone when

you wake up, so you don't have to lie and tell them you want to see them again, when you really don't." Char smiled. "Do I have that right?"

Christ, she was hard on him. He couldn't deny it. "Mostly, yes," Casey admitted. "You know me well. Or at least my reputation. But maybe not anymore. I got your note. I think I understand what you were trying to do. You wanted to get out of there early, spare yourself the rejection."

"Bingo," Char said. "Yet here I am. I must be a glutton for punishment."

Her insecurities were setting in again, and Casey knew he'd have to work hard to combat those. "I'm glad you are, because I want to see you again."

"Great, you're seeing me," Char said, although she picked up her menu, partially concealing her face with it as she studied it. Or pretended to, in order to avoid eye contact.

Casey reached over and pulled it down. "Not like that. Not like this. What I meant was, I want to *see* you again," he said, his voice earnest. "As in a date. A real one. Not just for sex." Was he even saying that? Oh, man. This was getting too real.

"I thought you didn't do those," Char said with a knowing smirk.

"I don't, but I'll make an exception for you," Casey said.

"Why?" She challenged.

He barely contained his sigh. She was a tough one, for sure. "Haven't I already told you why? I think you're sexy. Hot. Intriguing. I can't stop thinking about you," he said. "Isn't that enough?"

Char shook her head. "You make a tempting

offer, but it's a bad idea. It'll never work."

"Why?" Casey wanted to know. "Why are you so quick to say that? Is it all because of my reputation?"

"Partly, yes..."

"Okay, and the age thing?"

Char nodded. "Obviously. I'm forty years old, Casey. And you're—"

"Twenty-four, as of two months ago," he said.

"Exactly. Which I guess makes me a cougar."

"Does it? I mean, technically, I pursued you." He waved his hand. "Either way, it doesn't make any difference. At least not to me. These things can work. Look at Ashton and Demi."

"Yeah, look at 'em. They're divorced now, in case you didn't know."

Casey sighed. She had him there. "Fine. Ellen and Portia, then."

"Not the same thing. They're both women."

"I'm aware of that, yes." He didn't see that it mattered, either. His point was the same. "Fine. If that's how you want to play, I present Hugh Jackman. Happily married to a woman thirteen years his senior, and for two decades." Casey gave her a satisfied smile. Surely she had no snappy retort to that one.

"Yes, and they're a lovely couple. I'm not marrying you, Casey."

Or maybe she did. "And I didn't ask," he said. "All I'm asking is that you go on a date with me. Once, a real date. A chance to see if there's anything between us but really incredible sex. What do you say?" he asked. "Can you honestly tell me you haven't wondered that very thing?"

***

An hour later, Char left Luigi's with her stomach full of lasagna and a date for later that night, since Casey claimed lunch didn't count as a date. Funny, that was exactly what he'd called it when he first persuaded her to agree to that. Was that his plan? To keep changing the rules?

If it was, Char couldn't complain. Although she still struggled to believe in the sincerity of his words—he was as much of a smooth talker as he was a skater—it was hard for Char to turn down the invitation. Her memories from two nights ago remained too vivid in her mind. No, she didn't think the relationship could last. Hell, who was she kidding? It wasn't a relationship. It was sex, albeit really good sex, and Char had little doubt that Casey would quickly tire of her and move on to someone younger. Probably much younger. But for now, at least for one more night, he wanted to see her again, and Char couldn't forget the way he'd made her feel the first time. His lips on hers; the warmth of his breath against her neck. His hands roaming her body, touching, feeling, pleasuring her with his fingers. Then, finally, the tremors that shook through her as he made her climax, over and over again. Was it so wrong to want to experience that one more time?

CHAPTER SEVEN

J essica smirked. "So, you invited your boy toy over for sex?"

"No. I invited Casey over for dinner," Char corrected, her voice firm.

"Right. You keep telling yourself that, if it helps." Jessica's eyes danced with amusement. "Dinner, and then sex."

Maybe. Hopefully. Probably, at least if Char had anything to say about it. She tried for a casual shrug, but knew she didn't pull it off. "I don't know. We'll see where things go."

Jessica rolled her eyes. "You don't fool me for a minute, Char Simmons. I've known you way too long."

Indeed, she had. They'd been freshmen at UTSA the same year, even though Char was ten years older, having gone to college after her marriage ended. They were paired together on a group project in an English class, and been friends ever since. Char could never pull anything over on Jessica, and it was foolish to even try. "Fine. Yes. I'm inviting Casey over with the expectation that it will lead to sex," she said without apology. "I got him plenty turned on the night before last, and given the opportunity, I think I can do it again."

"I'm sure you can," Jessica said. "That's not the point."

"Then what is? I thought you weren't going to judge me."

"I'm not. I want you to be happy, Char."

"Me too. And you know what? Right now, I am. I'm working my dream job, I make good money, and I have a nice house and a really nice car." A smile tugged at Char's lips. "And I have a twenty-four-old stud who can give me multiple orgasms. Two days ago, I had the first four things on that list, and I was still trapped in a depressed funk," she said. "Casey pulled me out of it."

"Good. I'm grateful to him for that," Jessica said, "but I'm still worried you might be headed for a fall. I mean, I'm sorry, but I have to be blunt here, because that's how I am. Where do you think this is leading, Char? Do you honestly think it can last?"

"Last? As in the long term?" Char laughed. "No. I have no delusions about that. It might all end tomorrow." Most likely, it would, but then again, she'd said that the other night, too. "At the moment, I'm fine with that, because I'm not sure I can handle more. I'm taking it one day at a time. Is that okay with you?" Not that she needed permission, or even approval, but it would be nice to have it.

Jessica nodded. "It's fine. Just don't get in too deep. And don't get hurt."

"I won't," she said. "I promise. I'm a big girl."

"Good." Jessica laughed. "Because if Casey hurts you, I might have Ryder hurt him... and that will really derail our Stanley Cup chances."

"Not happening." Char joined her in laughing. "The Cup above all." She gave Jessica a hug. "Thank you. For being my friend and for being you. Now get the hell out of here before my boy toy gets here."

"Aha!" Jessica clapped her hands. "You just called him your boy toy."

"Yes, I did, and what of it? Are you leaving now?"

"Going." Jessica opened the door. "Have fun tonight. And call me tomorrow."

"I will," Char promised, closing the door behind her. She busied herself with straightening up the house and set chicken out to thaw for dinner, but didn't start preparing anything, in case she and Casey got distracted when he got there. And who was she fooling? Char hoped they got distracted.

Fifteen minutes later, the doorbell rang, and Casey stood there, dressed in jeans and a black sweater, and holding a holding a bouquet of flowers. "For you," he said, holding them out to her.

"Wow. You bring flowers to women, too?" Char regretted the words as soon as they were out. Talk about cynical. But Casey didn't seem to take offense.

"Not often, but I decided to make an exception for you."

"Thank you." Char took the flowers from him and carried them to the kitchen, where she filled a vase with water and set them on the table. "Can I give you a tour of the house?"

Casey nodded. "I'd like that."

"Okay." Char decided to throw caution to the wind. "I think we should start with the bedroom, if that's okay with you."

"Baby, I like the way you think."

***

Casey planned to exercise restraint, and be on his best behavior. He wanted to show Char he was serious, or that he could be. He wasn't only interested in the next lay.

Then she had to go and look totally hot, and suggested they start the tour of her house in the bedroom. If that wasn't an invitation, Casey didn't know what was. And how was he supposed to say no when she looked so damn hot? 'No' didn't tend to be in his vocabulary when it came to women and sex. At least this time, he'd managed to hold off on his climax until Char reached hers. It wasn't easy, but it was worth it to see the passion in her eyes.

An hour later, dressed in only his boxers, Casey sat on a chair in the kitchen, while Char fixed dinner. He'd offered to help, even though he was hopeless when it came to cooking, but she declined. Instead, he sat nursing a glass of white wine, while Char bustled about, wearing only a short kimono-style robe that she didn't cinch very tight. When she moved a certain way, Casey got a glimpse of her breasts. Christ. Was she trying to get him hard again? Because it wouldn't take much effort.

Finally, Char set the dish in the oven and joined him at the table, pouring herself a glass of wine. "It'll be ready in about twenty minutes," she said.

"Great. What are we having?"

"Chicken Parmesan. I figured that was okay, even if we just had Italian for lunch."

"Fine. It sounds great."

"While we wait, I thought we'd try to get to know each other a little bit."

Casey's mouth twitched. "Haven't we already done that?"

"That's not what I meant." Was it his imagination, or did Char blush? "We need to learn more about each other, see if we have anything in common. So I'll ask you a question, you answer, then ask me something. Deal?"

He nodded. "Sounds okay." A little silly, perhaps, but okay. "Go for it."

"Do you speak French?" Char asked.

"Fluently."

"Can you say something for me?"

Technically, that was two questions, but he didn't protest. "*Tu es très belle.*"

"What does that mean?"

"You're very beautiful."

"You don't mean that," Char demurred.

"You're wrong. I very much do," Casey insisted. "It's my turn now, though. What's your favorite movie?"

Char didn't hesitate to answer. "*Speed.*"

"The one with Sandra Bullock?" Yeah, it was official. He was falling hard.

"Yes. I'm surprised you've heard of it. Wasn't it released before you were born?"

"Very funny." Casey didn't laugh. "For the record, it was two years later, but it's one of my favorite movies."

"I bet you just like Sandra Bullock," Char said.

Casey couldn't deny it. "Of course I do. She's

an incredibly hot older woman, much like yourself," he said. "But more than anything, I like how they decide in the end to start a relationship based purely on sex."

"They didn't decide that," Char countered. "Jack merely suggested it."

"Yes, and I think it was a good suggestion. Maybe we should try it." Casey grinned. "What do you say?"

"Don't push your luck." Char stood up. "I'm going to check on dinner."

Casey admired the view as she got up and walked across the kitchen.

***

Char rolled over and found the other side of the bed empty, just as she expected. Casey was gone. She'd gotten another night with him, though, and she would cherish it.

She sat up, rubbed her eyes, and looked around for the note. Surely Casey would leave one, right? The gentle kiss off.

Instead of a note, though, Char found Casey standing over the bed, staring down at her. She almost jumped out of her skin. "Jesus, Casey."

He gave her a sheepish smile. "Sorry. Didn't mean to scare you."

"I thought for sure you'd be gone."

He nodded. "Yeah, I know, but I wasn't going to leave without saying goodbye. I do have to go pretty quick, though, or I'll be late to practice."

"Then go," Char urged. She knew his fate if we were so much as five minutes late for practice. The

Generals' coach carried a hard line. "I don't want to be responsible for you being scratched for an important game."

"You won't be," he said. "Thanks for an incredible night. Dinner was great, and so was the rest of it."

Char ignored the heat rising to her cheeks. "It sure was. You're welcome, and thank you, too."

"You'll be at the game tonight, right?" he asked.

Char nodded. "I have to be. We're starting the toy drive tonight."

"Great. I hope I get a chance to see you." Casey leaned down and gave her a kiss on the forehead. "And when I do, I hope you'll be wearing this."

He tossed something on the bed before walking out. Char didn't call after him, not wanting him to be late. Instead, she reached for it, knowing right away what it was.

Casey's number nineteen Generals jersey. If she wore it, Char knew she'd be making a statement. Casey might want her to, but was she ready?

MICHELE SHRIVER

CHAPTER EIGHT

After conducting an internal debate with herself over wearing the jersey, complete with a risk-benefit analysis worthy of a medical decision, Char opted for yes. Yes, she would wear Casey's jersey to the hockey game, and face the barrage of questions from the rest of the women.

Not surprisingly, it began as soon as they had all gathered in the arena concourse to set up for the toy drive. And even less surprising, it was led by Jessica. "Nice jersey," she said with a smirk to go along with her raised eyebrow. "And lucky number nineteen, even."

Char tried to downplay it with an exaggerated shrug. "It's nothing. I just want to do my part to support the team."

Meryl Johnson, the daughter of the Generals' owner, and the director of the team's youth and community initiatives, laughed. "That's exactly what I tried to tell people when I wore Nik's jersey to last year's toy drive, and no one believed me. Including you, Char."

It was true. Meryl had raised plenty of eyebrows the year before by donning the jersey of the team's young Russian superstar, Nikolai Brantov. It was a bold move, considering they weren't dating at the time, but they had been ever since, proving that Meryl's public declaration of interest had paid dividends. At the time, Char admired Meryl's individuality and willingness to take risks, especially compared to her own tendency to always play things safe. Then again, Meryl was twenty years younger than Char and the daughter of a billionaire. It was probably easier for her to take risks.

"It really is nothing," Char insisted. "Casey asked me to wear it, and I decided I would."

"He 'asked' you? Okay, *chica*, what are you not telling us?" Maya Dominguez demanded. She was a sports reporter, and engaged to the team captain, Colton Tremblay.

"Nothing."

"Okay, that's the third nothing," Angie Rollins said. "Not that I'm counting or anything, but three nothings usually mean something."

"Fine. Y'all are relentless." Char rolled her eyes. "Casey and I have been spending some together the past couple days, and he asked me to wear his jersey tonight. I figured 'what the heck?' It doesn't have to be a big thing."

"Except that it is," Jessica said. "The next step will be to make it Facebook official."

"Shut up." Char glared at her best friend.

"You and Casey. Oh, my. *¿Me estás tomando el pelo?*"

Char spoke fluent Spanish, and knew exactly

what Maya had said. She sighed. "No, I'm not kidding, but can you please not make a big deal out of this? Because it doesn't have to be."

"Relax, hon." Jessica put an arm around her. "We're only giving you a hard time because we love you."

"That's right," Angie said. "And we love Casey, too. If you're the woman who can finally succeed in taming him, then more power to you, and you will have our full support."

Char believed it, and appreciated it, but sensed they were all skeptical. Then again, she had her own doubts, and plenty of them. Yet she persisted anyway, even taking the bold step of wearing Casey's jersey in public, for reasons she didn't completely understand herself. At least none of them expected an explanation she couldn't give. "Thank you, but right now I'm more interested in you helping me get this table set up."

"Yes, boss," Meryl teased.

"In a second." Jessica held up her phone. "I need a picture first."

"What are you doing?" Char demanded, when she realized Jessica had just taken a picture. Of her. In Casey's jersey. "Don't you dare send that to Ryder."

"Too late." Jessica laughed as she slipped her phone back in her purse. "With a little luck, he'll show that to your boy toy before they take the ice, and he'll have a little extra motivation tonight."

"Let's hope so," Maya agreed. "We need the win."

"True." If seeing her in his jersey gave Casey a little extra motivation, then Char wouldn't complain.

***

Casey was guilty of the occasional bragging about his conquests to his teammates, but he'd kept mum about Char. He respected her position within the Generals organization, and he wasn't going to broadcast anything public if she wasn't ready. Hopefully he hadn't pushed her beyond her comfort level by suggesting she wear his jersey tonight.

"Hey, Case, look at this." Casey glanced over toward the locker stall next to his, where Ryder held his phone out. "Looks like you have an admirer."

Casey peered at the screen. It was Char, looking hot as usual, and sporting a maroon and gray Generals jersey. Although the picture was taken from the front, and his name wasn't visible on the back of the jersey, Casey could make out the number nineteen on the sleeve. "Well, I'll be damned. She actually wore it."

Ryder gave him a puzzled look. "You expected her to?"

"Not expecting, exactly, but I asked her to." Casey concentrated on his skates.

"Something you're not telling me?" Ryder asked. "When did you see Char?"

"Last night, for dinner." *And this morning, too.*

"What? Since when are you two friends?"

Casey shrugged. "Since a few nights ago, at her birthday party. The one you invited me to. Is that okay?"

Ryder didn't answer right away. "Depends. You're not going to hurt her, are you? Because she's Jessica's best friend."

"Like I don't know that?" Casey already didn't

like where this conversation was headed. "What makes you so quick to assume I'm going to hurt her?" He stood up and pulled his jersey over his pads.

"Hey, man, chill. I'm not assuming anything. Just saying, be careful."

Casey nodded. "Got it. No need to worry."

"Good. Then let's go kick some Ducks ass tonight."

The team headed out of the locker room, down the tunnel, and on to the ice for pregame warm-ups. Plenty of fans were gathered at glass level to watch the warm-ups, and it looked like it would be a packed house. Casey wanted to put on a show, especially since he knew Char was in the building. He looked to the area where the players' wives and girlfriends always sat, but the section was mostly empty. They were still out in the concourse working the toy drive.

Casey finished a lap around the rink, and assumed his position to take practice shots. Hopefully he'd be feeling his shot again tonight and he could pot a goal or two. And he hoped Char would be watching when he did.

***

Char watched the first two periods of the game on a video monitor in the concourse while manning the Foundation table. It meant she didn't have the greatest view of Casey's two goals. When the third period began, Meryl insisted on taking over, sending Char to the seats in the arena's lower bowl to watch the rest of the game.

"Your guy has the magic touch," she said. "Go cheer him on. Maybe he'll get the hat trick."

Char decided not to protest either the reference to Casey being her 'guy' or the offer of help so she could watch the remainder of the game from the stands. Instead, she happily took a seat in row eight as the third period began, with the score tied at two.

"Okay, bring Casey the good luck so we can finish this in regulation," Jessica said. "Ryder and I have a date."

Char didn't want to think about what Casey's post-game plans might be. No. She wasn't going to go there. "As if I have anything to do with it?"

Jessica shrugged. "You never know. It's hard to argue with the way he's played since you two hooked up."

Hooked up. Yeah. That's exactly what it was. So why was she here, wearing his jersey, and risking embarrassment and rumor by doing so? Char didn't get the chance to analyze further, because Casey took a beautiful pass from Ryder and buried it past the Ducks goalkeeper, giving the Generals a 3-2 lead. With the hat trick, the fans in the arena tossed their hats onto the ice.

As Casey skated over to the bench to celebrate with his teammates, he glanced a few rows behind the bench, locking his eyes with Char. She smiled at him, and he blew her a kiss.

There were squeals and sighs around her, from female fans who wanted to believe the kiss was intended for them. Char had little doubt, though, that it was directed at her, and she couldn't help but blush.

"Yeah, I'd say you're a good influence on him," Maya remarked. "Please, keep it up."

Casey's goal stood as the game winner, and as the final seconds expired, Char got up. "I need to go see about wrapping up the toy drive and getting everything put away in storage until Tuesday's game."

"I'll come help you," Jessica said.

"You don't have to. You said you have a date."

"Yeah, but Ryder won't be ready for a while," she said. "Hey, I have an idea. Let me send him a text and tell him to invite Casey. You guys can come with us."

"You can't be serious."

"Dead serious. C'mon, it'll be fun."

After a second's hesitation, Char shrugged. "Sure, I guess, if Ryder can get him to come along." Why not? The proverbial cat was already out of the bag, anyway. If he agreed, she'd have a better idea what Casey's intentions were.

MICHELE SHRIVER

CHAPTER NINE

The locker room was full of high-fives and congratulations, and after scoring the hat trick, Casey was the man of the hour. He wasn't certain whether it was a coincidence or not, but the scoring slump he was in a couple weeks ago ended once Char came into the picture. Now, if he could persuade her to stay in the picture, and not only because he liked the impact she had on his game.

"Any big plans tonight, Case?" Ryder asked.

"Not really." His post-game routine had changed, and Casey wondered if he could get back to it, or if he even wanted to. Tonight he had no desire to. He also didn't want to go straight home to an empty apartment. "You?"

"Jess and I are going out for a late dinner, and she texted me, said to invite you." He gave Casey a wink. "Sounds like she's trying to persuade Char to come along, too."

"Is that right?" Casey perked up. Could Ryder and Jessica actually be allies for him? He hadn't expected it, but he wouldn't complain. "Then that sounds great. Where are you going?" Not that it mattered. If Char was there, it was where Casey intended to be.

"Don't know yet." Ryder shrugged. "Food, drinks, we'll figure something out. I just want to be with my girl. She doesn't get to come to many games with her work schedule."

Casey smiled into the mirror as he knotted his tie and smoothed down his damp hair. "Yeah, me too." His girl. Singular. What the hell happened that he liked the sound of that?

They left the locker room and made their way up to the concourse. The arena was almost empty now, except for workers cleaning up after the game and security personnel. Casey wasn't used to walking through it after games, and found it to be a different environment. They got to the Foundation table where Char and Jessica and a few others were working to take everything down.

Ryder greeted Jessica with a kiss, and Casey longed to do the same to Char, but he didn't know how she would react, so he kept it casual. "Hi."

"Hello, Mr. Hat Trick," she said with a grin. She no longer wore his jersey, much to Casey's disappointment. Instead, Char was dressed in a gray sweater and jeans that perfectly hugged her hips. "Great game."

"Thank you. The shots just seem to be finding the back of the net lately." He shrugged. "Maybe it's luck." *And maybe you're bringing it.* That's the way it seemed, anyway.

"You're too modest," Char said. "So are we headed out somewhere to celebrate?"

"That's the plan," Ryder said. "What about

Southerleigh? It's open late."

"Sounds good." Casey nodded in Char's direction. "What do you say?"

"Works for me." Char slipped on a black leather coat, lifting her hair up, giving Casey a glimpse of her neck—which he longed to kiss—before releasing it and letting it fall past her shoulders. If he found that gesture to be incredibly sexy—and he did—it was a sure sign that he was headed for trouble. Big trouble. He didn't mind.

"Want a ride in my Mustang, Hat Trick?" Char asked. "I think I promised you one."

"You did, yes. Now's as good a time as any to cash in." Casey turned to Ryder. "We'll meet you there," he said, putting his arm around Char's shoulder.

***

It was a cool night, but not too cold, so put the top down on the Mustang. "I hope you don't mind. I love the feel of the wind blowing through my hair."

"I don't mind at all. You can't do this in Canada in December," Casey said. "Besides, you'll look sexy with the wind blowing through your hair."

Char laughed as she turned her head to look at him. "Don't I *always* look sexy?"

Casey grinned. "Of course you do, baby. That's a given."

She backed the car out of the parking place. Casey was so good for her ego. It may not last. It probably wouldn't last. But right here, right now, he made her feel good. That was all Char cared about. The future would take care of itself. "Do you like to go fast?" she asked as they exited the arena parking lot and headed toward the interstate.

"Do you even have to ask?"

Char laughed as she hit the accelerator. "I knew there was a reason I liked you."

It was a short drive to Southerleigh, a fine dining restaurant and brewery that Char had been to once before, and the feel of the wind blowing her hair was exhilarating. Sure, it was probably messy now, but she didn't care and she doubted Casey did.

"I can see why you love this car," he said as she eased it to a stop.

"Sweet little machine, isn't it?" She didn't even have the chance to open her door before Casey rushed around to help her out. "Nice." She gave him a smile of approval. "Is this your romantic side?" He was full of surprises.

"Hey, I may be a playboy, but I can do romance, too." Casey reached for her hand. "You bring out the best in me. Especially on the ice tonight."

Char laughed. "Yeah, the rest of the girls are hoping you'll keep me around for a bit."

"Funny, because I'm hoping to persuade you to stick around for a bit."

"I know you are." Char relaxed against him. "I'm still not sure about that, but so far, you're making all the right moves."

Ryder and Jessica hadn't arrived yet, so they got a table while they waited. "Do you like craft beer?" Casey asked.

Char nodded. "Yes. You?"

"Sure do." He smiled. "Why? Does that surprise you? Were you thinking because I'm young, I can't have taste?"

"Oh, honey, I know you have taste." Char winked at him. "You're here with me, aren't you?"

Casey laughed. "Touché."

It turned out he did know his craft beer, ordering the Darwinian IPA, while Char opted for Bill & Red's Excellent Lager. "I prefer the maltier ones," she said by way of explanation.

"Works for me. I always suspected you were a woman of fine taste.

"Of course I am, which is why I'm here with you." Char leaned over and kissed him.

"Okay, you two, enough with the PDA." Jessica's tone was teasing.

"Oh, bite me," Char said. "We had to do something while we waited. It took you long enough to get here."

"Because some of us don't drive as fast, or have such fancy cars," Jessica said, as she and Ryder sat down on the opposite side of the table. "Did you guys order already?"

Char shook her head. "Just drinks." She picked up the menu. "I'm starving, though, and I'm sure Hat Trick here is, after the game he played."

*   *   *

Casey didn't know what changed, or when, but Char was no longer shy about flirting with him, and he liked it. When he was with her, he never thought about the age difference. Why should he? They fit so well together.

She was a bit of a foodie, he concluded, because she knew exactly what she wanted. She was also picky, or not crazy about big entrées, because she ordered three sides. Jalapeño white cheddar grits, old fashioned cornbread, and Gulf crab macaroni and cheese. Casey had to admit it sounded rather tasty, but he opted for the chicken fried alligator.

"Seriously, you're going to eat an alligator?" Char asked.

"I am," Casey said. "Why? Does that offend you? Are you on a save the alligator mission?" He didn't think so, because the twinkle in her green eyes told him she was teasing.

"Nope." She winked. "I want to try some, see if it actually does taste like chicken."

"Consider it done." Was it crazy that he wanted to kiss her again, right here in front of everyone? Hell, who was he kidding? He always wanted to kiss her.

"Aren't you two cute?" Jessica asked.

"We try," Char answered. "Now, is anyone getting the crispy chicken cracklins? Because I want to taste those, too."

Yep. Definite foodie, and since the restaurant served family style, the arrangement worked well. They rounded things out with a gulf redfish, with everyone sampling each, and by the time they left, after polishing off dessert s'mores with dark chocolate, Casey was glad he was young and had a fast metabolism.

"I guess you're not one of those salad only type of girls," he said to Char as they left the restaurant.

"What makes you say that? Are you saying I'm fat?"

Christ! Is that what she thought? So much for being good with women. "No, God no. I think you're hot as hell. Isn't that obvious?"

"Pretty much." Char laughed. "I was joking, but I think I had you for a minute."

"You did, yeah." Casey let out a sigh of relief. "Whew. Here I'm trying to convince you I'm worth spending time with. I can't do that if I'm offending you."

"Relax, you're fine." Char gave him kiss as they arrived at her car, then walked around to the driver's side. "To answer your question, no I'm not a salad kind of girl. Food is a passion of mine, and this a great city for food. You only live once, and realistically, half of my life is about over. I intend to enjoy myself."

"Works for me." It made sense to Casey, and he realized he operated with similar philosophy. He was young, yes, and sometimes felt invincible, but he also knew it could all end at any time. So why not have as many women as he could? It seemed like a solid approach to life, at least until about a week ago.

They drove in silence back to the arena, mainly because they couldn't carry on much of a conversation on the highway with the top down. Char pulled into the parking lot, next to Casey's BMW, and he assumed he'd follow her back to her house, or she'd follow him to his place. Instead, she said, "Thanks for the late dinner. Call me tomorrow?"

Casey was caught off guard, and unsure how to respond. "I could, yeah, or..." his voice trailed off. She'd get the hint, right?

"Nope." Char shook her head. "If you're going to convince me you're serious about where this is headed, we're slowing things down," she said. "And Casey?"

"What?"

"If you ever want to see me again, outside of a professional capacity, you better go straight home and sleep alone. I meant that. No screwing around."

She meant it, all right. Her tone said it all. "I got it," Casey said. "I'll show you. I am serious." He leaned over and kissed her. "I've never known anyone like you, and I want to know more." He opened the passenger door and let himself out. It would suck spending the night alone, but it was time to change. Char was worth it.

***

She'd been home less than ten minutes when the phone rang. Char expected it might be Jessica, ready to grill her about Casey. No, she was probably still with Ryder, so that would have to wait until morning. Instead, the call was from Casey.

"Hey," she greeted as she answered. "What's up?"

"You said to call tomorrow, but I didn't want to wait," Casey said. "I'm home now. Alone. Watching the weather."

Char laughed. "Sounds fascinating."

"For sure," Casey said. "Do you want me to prove what I'm doing?"

Was he serious? Char settled back onto the couch. It was late, and she should go to bed, but she was still too wound up to sleep. "It's not necessary. I trust you." And oddly enough, she did. "How did you plan on proving it, though? Just out of curiosity."

"Like this." The line went quiet for a minute,

and then Char heard the sound of a television blaring at maximum volume. Yes, it sounded like a weather report. It lasted long enough to get the forecast—seventy two degrees—then Casey was back on the line. "Did you hear that?"

"I did, yes. Sounds like tomorrow's going to be a beautiful day."

"I know. Hard to believe it's December. What are you doing tomorrow?"

"Working," Char said. "Same ole, same ole."

"Can you take any time off? Like in the afternoon?"

Char mentally reviewed her schedule. She didn't have any appointments scheduled for the next day, and she'd been putting in a lot of long hours leading up to the toy drive. Maybe she *should* take an afternoon off. "I suppose. Why?"

"Because I want to see you," Casey said. "Is that a good enough reason?"

"It works, yeah."

"Great. I've got an optional skate in the morning, but I'm going to it. Then it's a free day. How about noon? I can come to your office."

Char hesitated. Was it a good idea for him to come to her office, or would it start rumors? And if it did, was she prepared to handle it? "Can I meet you somewhere?"

"No," Casey said. "I'm not sure where we're going yet, and I want to see what you do. I told you I want to get to know you better."

He had, yes, and he seemed genuine about it. Maybe it was time to bury her skepticism and go along for the ride. "Okay," Char said. "Come to my office.

I'll see you then."

"Thanks. Good night, sexy. Sweet dreams."

"You too, Hat Trick." Char smiled as she ended the call. Yes, she'd have very sweet dreams, indeed.

CHAPTER TEN

After a hard-fought victory, the team's morning skate wasn't mandatory. Casey never skipped optional skates, but for the first time he considered it, if it would mean he could spend the entire day with Char. He was superstitious, though, and didn't want to do anything to change his routine, especially when he was on such a scoring streak. As a result, he was at the rink bright and early. Not surprisingly, the ultra-competitive Ryder was already there. He never missed a skate, either, unless he was injured.

"Question for you," Casey said as he put on his gear. "How well do you know Char?"

Ryder smirked. "Not as well as you do, obviously."

"Oh, you're funny," Casey said, but didn't laugh.

"Why? Is something wrong? I thought things were getting pretty hot and heavy between the two of you."

"Maybe, sort of," Casey said. "I mean, there's a connection, for sure. But I'd like more, and she seems, I don't know, reluctant or something. Like she doesn't believe I'm serious, or she doesn't quite trust me. I wondered if you knew anything."

"You mean like her relationship history?"

Casey nodded. "Yes, that."

Ryder frowned. "Hmm. I don't know. I think Jess said something about her being married once, a long time ago, but I don't know any details."

"Hmm." Casey thought about it. "So she's divorced. That might explain it."

"Explain what?"

"Why she seems skeptical of relationships."

"Maybe," Ryder said. "But if you have considered another reason? Like perhaps you're the problem?"

"Gee, thanks." Casey glared at him. "What's that supposed to mean?"

"Do you even have to ask? Um, let's see. How do I put this delicately, since you seem to be easily offended this morning?" Ryder put a finger to his chin. "You don't exactly have a history of being, well, monogamous."

Casey slumped into his seat. "Fair enough, but I've never had a good reason why I'd want to be." Maybe it was shallow, or selfish, or whatever, but it was the truth. He was young, rich, and successful. He liked women, and women liked him. Why shouldn't he be allowed to play the field? At least it seemed like a good enough philosophy a week ago.

"Are you saying you do now?" Ryder's expression was dubious. "That you're done banging anything in a skirt, no matter how cheap and sleazy they are, and you're ready to be with only one woman, and you want that woman to be Char?"

Was that what he was saying? Casey thought about the scene at the bar a few nights ago. Wynter, with her cheap perfume that didn't mask the odor of cigarettes and whiskey, rubbing against him, her intentions obvious. And instead of getting aroused and wanting to find the nearest surface to screw her on, he wanted to get away from her and go home. Alone. Where he'd spent a restless night thinking about Char. "Yeah." Casey stood up and raked a hand through his hair. "That's what I'm saying. I just need to find a way to convince Char and everyone else that I'm serious, and that maybe this is real."

***

Since she committed herself to taking the afternoon off, Char went to the office bright and early, ready to pore through the latest donation reports. She was a third of the way through them when Jessica called.

"Good morning, sunshine," Char greeted her.

"Wow. You sound like you're in a good mood this morning."

Char leaned back in her chair and sipped coffee from her favorite Generals mug. "As a matter of fact, I am. We've had a record setting December, and that doesn't even include the donations from last night. *And* we still have two more games of the toy drive," she added with a satisfied smile.

"Congratulations," Jessica said. "Here I thought your cheerfulness might be the result of how you spent your night."

"Oh, such a comedian. For your information, I

spent the night alone."

"Really?" Jessica's tone changed. "Did something happen after you and Casey left the restaurant? Because you seemed to be having a good time."

"We had a great time," Char said. "It could've been even better, but I decided to think with my brain, so I sent Casey home alone." She took another drink of coffee. "He wants me, there's not doubt about that, and it's a very nice feeling. I want to make him work for it a little, though."

"Good for you," Jessica said. "I have to admit you're kind of cute together, and it's nice to see you smiling and laughing, but..." Her voice trailed off.

"But what?"

"I don't know. Maybe I'm cynical, but in twenty years, you'll be—"

"Sixty," Char said, flinching slightly. Good grief. She'd barely adjusted to forty, and here Jess was trying to push sixty on her. "And Casey will be forty-four. I aced math and I work with numbers every day. I got it."

"Sorry," Jessica said."I didn't mean to upset you."

"I'm not upset, and I know you mean well," Char said. "I get that the numbers are ugly."

"But at the moment, you don't care."

That was it. In a nutshell. "Yep. Bingo. He persuaded me to take this afternoon off. I have no idea yet where we're going, and I don't care about that, either."

"I'm glad," Jessica said. "You work too hard."

"That I do. Thirteen hours yesterday, counting

the game. But you know what? Today I'm giving myself permission to have fun." Char looked at her watch. "In about three hours."

Jessica laughed. "Then I'll let you go. And Char?"

"Yes, sunshine?"

"I meant what I said. I think you and Casey are cute together. Don't let my skepticism make you think otherwise."

"Oh, don't worry. I wouldn't. I think we're pretty cute together myself." Char smiled. *Pretty cute, indeed.* "I'll talk to you later, okay?" She added before ending the call.

She worked the rest of the morning without a break, until her assistant knocked on her door and came in.

"Casey Denault is here to see you," Leah announced. "From the team."

Char almost laughed at the needless clarification. "Yes, I know who he is." *I know very well.*

Leah nodded. "He says you have an appointment, and you're going to tell him more about the work we do here."

Good, job, Casey. Char nodded. "Yes, that's right. Send him in."

A moment later, Casey walked in, dressed in jeans and an untucked blue button down shirt, and looking impossibly gorgeous. Also very, very young. It was pretty hard to get past that.

"Hey." Casey walked toward her, then turned back around. Satisfied that the door was closed and they didn't have an audience, he put his arms around her and pulled her into a kiss. "Are you ready to go, or would you rather I just have my way with you right here on your desk?"

His gray-blue eyes twinkled in amusement, letting Char know he kidded her. The offer intrigued her, though.

"You do know how to tempt me. We better get out of here before I decide to take you up on that." Char rounded her desk and picked up her purse from underneath it, swinging it over her shoulder. "Leah says you told her you're here to learn more about the Foundation's work. That's pretty clever."

Casey gave a shrug, then placed an arm around Char's shoulder. "I try. And if anyone asks, we'll say it was a working lunch."

"Perfect," Char said, but as she nestled her body against his, Casey's arm moved lower, until it was no longer around her shoulder, but rather his hand had found the back pocket of her jeans. Yeah. *Working lunch, my ass.*

***

Although he would've much preferred to have his way with Char right there in her office, on her desk, Casey was happy to settle for a not-so-subtle grope of her ass as they walked to the elevator. That she allowed him that much was affirmation to Casey that he was making headway. But how much?

"I thought of something as I got here. You're not forbidden from dating me, are you?" He didn't know why the question occurred to him. Maybe it was the team name and logo on the sig and doors.

Char looked up at him, her expression amused.

"Is that what I'm doing now? Dating you?"

"Well, aren't you?" That she even questioned n didn't quite sit well with Casey. "I think we can safely say we've moved past the 'just a one-night stand' thing by this point." If she was wearing his jersey, and he was refraining from picking up other women, that better count for something.

"Yes," Char admitted. "I guess that means I can't call you my boy toy anymore." A smile tugged at her lips,

"Is that what you've been calling me?" Casey didn't know whether to be flattered or offended, so he straddled the line between both.

"Not me, so much. It was more Jessica's word for you," Char said. "She was teasing."

"Oh." Casey couldn't stop his mind from wondering what Char might have said about him to her best friend. "That's okay. I'm cool with being your boy toy, if that's how you want it. I aspire to more, though." They stopped beside his car, but he made no move to open it

"Good." Char chuckled. "I like a man with ambition. And to answer your question, no I'm not prohibited from dating you." She stood on her toes and gave him a kiss. "I just couldn't bid on a date with you at the charity auction, because it was a Foundation-sponsored event."

Casey nodded. "That makes sense," he said. "Though I wish you would've." Instead, he knew Char had used her money to set Jessica up with Ryder. Meanwhile, his date from the auction had been a disaster. "It's nice to know you wanted to bid on me."

"Who said that? I kind of had my heart set on

Trenton," Char deadpanned.

"Oh, you slay me." Casey put a hand to his chest. "I don't know if I can recover from these wounds."

"Dramatic much?" Char rolled her eyes. "Tell me if this helps," she said, and kissed him again."

It helped, all right, and much like the first time when they'd shared a kiss, Casey didn't want it to end. He pulled away with reluctance. "That's a very good start, and I fully intend to come back to it later," he said. "But I have other things planned first." He pressed the key fob to unlock his car, then walked around to open the passenger door for Char. "Your chariot awaits. I hope this isn't too much of a letdown from that machine you drive."

"I think this'll do just fine," she said, running a hand along door before getting in. "You haven't said where you're taking me, though."

"Oh, that." Casey grinned. "Six Flags Fiesta Texas."

CHAPTER ELEVEN

C har figured her jaw dropped when Casey said they were going to the amusement park. It was the last thing she expected, but she was game. No way did she want him thinking she lacked a spirit of adventure.

Before Six Flags, though, they stopped for lunch at a street vendor specializing in Chicago style hot dogs.

"I hope this is okay," Casey said. "There was a place like this not too far from where I lived when I played for the Blackhawks."

"It's fine." Char laughed. "I think we already established that I love my food." She decided against the traditional Chicago style, though, and instead ordered hers loaded up with chili, cheese, and jalapeño peppers.

"Oh, hot food for a hot girl, huh?" Casey said, a smile playing at his lips.

"Yep. I like things spicy, and I'm not talking only about food." She gave him a wink as she bit into the hot dog. It tasted delicious, and she washed it down with a swallow of Dr. Pepper. "You can't live in San

Antonio for your entire life and not develop a taste for the spicier side of life."

"I suppose. I'm still working on that." Casey opted for the true Chicago style, with mustard, sweet green pickle relish, onions, a dill pickle spear, tomato wedges, two sport peppers, and celery salt, all on a poppy-seed bun.

Char had never eaten a hot dog like that, and doubted she'd like it, but to each their own. "You haven't been here long, so you might still acquire a taste for the hot stuff," she said. "Do you miss Chicago?"

Casey shrugged. "Maybe a little, but I only played there for a year," he said. "I like San Antonio a lot. You can't beat sitting outside getting food from a street vendor a few days before Christmas."

"True. I bet it's completely different from Canada." Char licked chili from her lip. "Ottawa's home, right?"

He nodded. "Yep. Do you know where all of us are from, or am I just special?"

"Oh, you're definitely special, Casey," Char said. "I've tried to learn as much about all of you guys as I can. It helps me think up new projects. I'm working my dream job, and I want to do it right."

"So what did you do before the Generals? Have you always been a hockey fan?"

Char shook her head. "No. Hockey is new, but I'm a fast learner, and it's consumed me." She'd gone from knowing nothing about the sport to practically obsessing over it, and if this thing with Casey continued, she'd probably be even more obsessed. "Let's see. I worked for the United Way when I first got out of college, then I took a position with the WNBA team here. That's what got me into the sports side of things, and I realized that's where I want to be, so when the Generals came to town, I applied." She took another drink of her Dr. Pepper. "And here I am."

"Well, I can't speak for anyone else, but I for one am glad of that." Casey finished the last bite of his hot dog and wiped his mouth. "I'm very glad I met you, Char Simmons."

He leaned over and kissed her, and Char tasted a hint of relish and onions. Even that was appealing on him. "I'm glad I met you, too, Casey Denault. I have no idea where this is going, but I sure am enjoying the ride."

***

It occurred to Casey that perhaps he should've asked first whether Char was up for a visit to Fiesta Texas. Not everyone liked amusement parks. What if she didn't, and he'd made a huge mistake? He chalked it all up to his lack of experience with the dating thing. When all he was interested in was getting a woman into his bed, he never paid any attention to compatibility or common interests, or anything like that. Sex was enough of a common interest, and he never had to work very hard to get a woman to sleep with him. Hell, who was he kidding? He didn't have to work at all.

Now Char made him work for things, and Casey realized he liked it. He liked the challenge, and he wanted to find new ways to show her a good time. But as he paid the admission at the amusement park, Casey began to second guess his choices for the day.

Hot dogs and theme parks? Char was a mature, classy, sophisticated woman. Was he only highlighting his youth and immaturity in bringing her here? Maybe he should've asked one the older guys on the team, or better yet, their wives, for dating advice.

"Are you sure this is okay with you?" he asked. "Because if it's not, we can always go somewhere else."

"After you've already paid?" Char shook her head. "No, Casey, this is fine. Perfect, really. I've been too on edge lately, first with the stupid birthday and now all of my end of year projects. I need to relax and put it all out of my head, and this should do the trick," she said. "In fact, I want you to take me on the scariest, most jaw-dropping ride in the park. Can you do that?"

Casey couldn't help but grin like an idiot. Yep. If there was any woman in the world worth changing his ways for, it was the one who stood in front of him, challenging him to scare her out of her wits. "You got it." Casey took Char's hand and headed in the direction of the park's information booth. "Excuse me," he said, "my girlfriend here wants to go on your scariest ride. Can you tell us what that is?"

"Hmm. You've got quite a few contenders," the pimply-faced teenager said. "Most people seem to think it's the Iron Rattler, our wooden and steel roller coaster. It's even got a 170 foot drop, at about seventy miles an hour, and four barrel rolls."

Casey wasn't a veteran of roller coasters, and didn't know what a barrel roll was, but if the Iron Rattler was the scariest ride in the park, then it was the ride they would start with. Unless Char had a change of heart after hearing the description, which wouldn't upset Casey too terribly much. He turned to her. "What do you say, babe?"

There wasn't even a flicker of hesitation in her eyes. "I say we go check out the Iron Rattler, and see if this guy's right."

The kid looked at Casey in awe. "You're lucky, man. I can't get my girlfriend to go anywhere near the Rattler."

Casey thanked him for the help, and left in search of the coaster.

"Your girlfriend, huh?" Char asked. "I guess that makes you my boyfriend."

"Well, yeah," Casey said. "We did establish that I'd moved beyond boy toy status."

"That's true." Char laughed. "And now you're the envy of that sixteen-year-old kid."

"Yep, and all because of you." At the moment, Casey felt like the luckiest guy in the world. "Not only are you sexy and smart, but you've got some serious balls, too." He chuckled. "In the figurative sense, of course."

***

Char felt far less ballsy and brave when she set eyes on the famous—or perhaps more appropriately, infamous—Iron Rattler. Maybe suggesting the scariest ride wasn't the smartest idea, but there was no way she would back out, not after she'd earned major cool points, both with Casey and the kid working at the information booth. No. She could do this.

Her heart raced as they took their place in the cart, and she closed her eyes, not wanting to look at the track ahead, with its steep drops and curves.

Casey gave her hand one final squeeze before placing it back on the safety bar in front of them. "Are you ready, babe."

"Ready." If she wasn't, it was too late, as the cart began to move. It began slowly, lulling Char into a false sense of security that maybe it wouldn't be so bad. Then came the huge drop, causing her to scream like a banshee, a scream which continued as they went through the pitch black tunnel. At least she was in good company, because Casey was screaming right along side her.

Her heart still beat too fast when they stepped out of the car at the end of the ride. Char could see why it earned the reputation as the park's scariest ride. If for some reason it wasn't, she didn't want to know what was.

"Yikes. I almost peed my pants," Casey said. "I'm not sure I'm brave enough for you."

"I'm not sure I'm brave enough for me, either."

Casey chuckled. "So you're saying you don't want to ride it again?"

Was it a challenge? "I think I need a drink first, then I might consider it."

"That sounds like a great idea."

They sat and drank a beer, then strolled hand in hand around the park before going on a few tamer rides. Char's favorite was the Hustler, which was a billiard balled themed take on the classic spinning tea cups that she had loved as a child. Char laughed harder than she had in years as they spun around in a giant billiard ball, then was so dizzy when they ride ended that she had a hard time standing up straight. She had no complaints, though, because she was having a great time.

"You're a heck of a good sport," Casey praised on the drive back.

"Maybe you just bring out my wild side," Char countered.

Casey pulled up beside her Mustang in the now nearly empty parking lot of the team offices. "Nice try, but any woman who drives a machine like that doesn't need any help being wild."

"Hmm. Could be." Char reached for the door handle. "Thanks, Casey. That was a lot of fun." The best part was she hadn't thought about work once, or dwelled at all on their burgeoning relationship, or what any of this might mean. She'd simply enjoyed Casey's company.

"Yes, it was," he said. "So, is this the part where I kiss you goodbye, and you send me on my way with an admonishment that I better behave myself tonight?"

Char hesitated, but only for about a millisecond. "No. This is the part where I ask you to meet me at my house, and behaving yourself is optional. In fact, I think I'd prefer if you don't."

Casey grinned. "Oh, babe, I like the way you think."

CHAPTER TWELVE

The last game of the Generals' homestand prior to the holiday break was a Saturday afternoon matinee. After that, the players got three days off before their next game, which happened to be a road game against the Ottawa Senators. When the season schedule was first released, Casey was thrilled with the way it worked out, since he planned to spend the Christmas break with his family in Ottawa. In meant he got a longer break than some of the guys, because he could meet the team there, rather than travel back to San Antonio only to have to turn around and fly again to their next game's destination. What looked good in June, though, wasn't as appealing now. Less flying would be nice. The time at home would be nice. Going five days without seeing Char was a lot less nice.

Casey wanted to spend as much time as possible with her before he left, but the team owner had other ideas about his schedule. Since the game featured an early afternoon start, Richard Johnson invited all of the players to his home for dinner afterward. Fortunately, Casey managed to persuade Char to attend with him, so he'd still be with her. He just wouldn't be *alone* with her.

The game ended in a 2-1 overtime loss to San Jose. Casey scored the Generals' lone goal, bringing his total to six during the three-game homestand. It was the best three-game scoring streak of Casey's career, and it coincided with Char. Even the rest of the guys were now joking that he needed to keep her around as his good luck charm.

The loss was disappointing, but at least they'd earned the overtime 'loser point' in the standings. Any and all points would help in the quest to earn the second consecutive playoff berth in team history. Casey wouldn't get too down about it. Not when he had so much to be happy about right now.

During the locker room remarks after the class, Coach Moreau and Colton tried to award Casey with the gun holster again. It would've marked the third game in a row, but when Colton reached out to hand it to him, Casey shook his head. "No. I'm not the player of the game. Sure, I scored, but not enough to win. We're all trying to pump each other up, saying we're glad we got the point. Well, that point was earned by Beck. How many shots did the Sharks take on us? Thirty-eight, I think." He might have been one or two off, but the result was the same. It had been an ugly game, and their goalie carried them on his back, and almost bailed them out.

"If not for Beck, we wouldn't have even gotten to overtime and had the chance at a win. We would've been behind 4-0 in the first period. As far as I'm concerned, Beck's the player of the game and gets to wear this." Casey took the holster from Colton and then passed it to their goalie. "Here you go, man. You more than earned this one."

The rest of the guys applauded as Beck took the holster from Casey. When it quieted down, Coach Moreau addressed them. "Classy move, Denault, and one of the reasons why I love coaching this team," he said. "Get ready, and I'll see all of you at Mr. Johnson's house a little later. And then after that, go and have a great holiday break. You've *all* earned it."

***

"Are you sure this is okay?" Char asked as they turned into the circular drive of Richard Johnson's sprawling estate. "Me being here with you?"

"Of course," he said. "Why wouldn't it be? You're my date."

"Yes... and I'm his employee." She couldn't help but feel awkward going to a dinner that her boss was hosting for the hockey team.

"So am I." Casey eased the car to a stop. "Besides, Seth is bringing Angie, Alex is bringing Kris. Maya's coming with Colton. And Meryl will be here."

"Meryl's his daughter, so that's not the same. And the others are married to your teammates, or at least engaged." She was about a week into this relationship, if that's what it even was. "They also don't work for him." Maybe her nerves were unfounded. She knew Ryder invited Jessica to attend as well, but she had to fill in for the weekend anchor at the news station on short notice.

"Relax. It'll be fine. He'll be glad to see you." Casey exited the car and rushed around to open her door for her. "Have I mentioned you look beautiful tonight?"

"Maybe once or twice, but who's counting?" The weather had turned chilly, at least compared to a couple days ago, so Char ditched the cocktail dress idea in favor of a black pencil skirt and an emerald green sweater with V-neck.

Casey linked his fingers through hers as they walked to the front door, which was opened by Rick Johnson himself. Char was surprised, having expected a member of his household staff. She knew he had one.

"Hello, Casey," he greeted. "And Charlene. Meryl told me you'd probably be joining us tonight."

At least he had some advance notice. "Yes. I hope you don't mind, sir."

"Not at all." He waved a dismissive hand. "And it's Rick."

"Okay." She smiled. "Then it's Char. Only my mother is allowed to call me Charlene, and only when she's mad at me."

"All right, then." The wealthy older man chuckled. "I wouldn't want to create any mistaken impression that I'm mad at you. On the contrary, I'm very pleased with the work you're doing with the Foundation. I hear the toy drive was a big success."

"It was, yes. We've also raised a lot of money from the cookbook sales," she said. "I'm still finishing up all of the last quarter reports, but I think we can expect a record-setting year." Char couldn't keep the pride from her voice. It might only be the second full year of the San Antonio Generals Foundation, but it had been a very successful one.

"Excellent. I'll be sure to mention that in my

remarks tonight," Rick said. "I want to make sure you get the recognition you deserve."

As Rick led them into the dining room, Casey leaned over and whispered in Char's ear. "See. I told you it'd be fine. He adores you. He doesn't mind at all that you're here."

It proved to be true, as Char felt very welcome in the team owner's home as the evening progressed. True to his word, Rick Johnson acknowledged her work with the Foundation, along with the accomplishments of all of the members of the team. Even though he had a reputation as being controlling and arrogant—and what billionaire didn't?—Char found him to be surprisingly genuine.

She also enjoyed getting to know some of the other members of the team a little better, as she hadn't had the opportunity to work with all of them directly before. By the time the evening ended, Char's mind was already turning, trying to come up with new charity projects that might be suited to some of the guys' individual interests.

For example, she learned Noah Mann was an avid golfer, and liked to play a round of mini-golf to relax before home games. "Do you think Noah might be interested in hosting a golf event for the foundation?" Char asked Casey as they walked out to his car after dinner. "Maybe a kid's event at the mini-golf course, or maybe even a local celebrity tournament at the country club?"

Casey chuckled as he unlocked the door. "You never stop working, do you?"

"That's not fair. Occasionally, I do," Char said. "Like when I'm with you. Tonight being the exception." With the whole team present, it was hard not to turn it into a working dinner of sorts.

"Hmm," Casey said. "I guess you need to spend more time with me, or you might be overworked."

"I might." Char gave him a flirtatious smile as she got in the car. "Any big plans for the rest of the night?"

Casey got in the driver's side, but leaned over and kissed her before starting the car. "Well, for starters, I'm driving you home. The rest is negotiable, depending on you."

Char had no intention of negotiating anything. Casey would be leaving for Ottawa in the morning and she wouldn't see him again for five days. "Oh, I think we can find some way to pass the time until you leave."

***

It was the best way Casey could've thought of to pass the time. In fact, as he lay next to Char, listening to her breath against his chest, it was very easy to imagine staying like this for a long time. He suddenly hated the thought that he had to leave her.

"I don't want you to go," Char said, as if reading his mind.

"That makes two of us."

"That's not true. You want to see your family."

Casey considered that, and nodded. "I do, yeah. I miss them. It's hard, sometimes, being so far away. So when you look at it that way, I do want to go. I hate leaving you, though." *I hate leaving this.*

He propped a pillow behind his head, sitting up a little bit. "How about you? What are you doing for

Christmas?" It occurred to Casey that he still knew very little about her. She'd said she'd spent her whole life in San Antonio, and he knew from Ryder that she'd been married once, and gone to college after her divorce, and that's where she met Jessica. And she'd devoted her life to working for charitable organizations, and liked food, especially spicy food. Beyond that, Char was a mystery. "Do you have any family around?" He hoped she wouldn't be spending the holiday alone. If she told him that, Casey might rethink his own plans.

Char rolled over to face him, resting her head in one hand. "My mom and my stepdad have a house up in Canyon Lake, just north of town. I'll drive up there tomorrow and spend a couple days with them. That's probably as long as I can stand." Char let out a chuckle that struck Casey as forced.

"You're not close to your mother?"

"Closer now than a few years ago," Char said. "Let's just say we have a complicated relationship. We always have. It's getting better, though. She's mellowed since she remarried."

Casey nodded, pleased that she'd begun to open up to him a little bit. "And your dad? Is he in the picture?"

"He lives in Florida. I see him a couple times a year," she said. "He's busy with wife number three."

Ouch. It must be a complicated history, too, and so different from Casey's own family life growing up. "Is that why you're cynical about relationships? Because you're a product of divorce and your dad's been married several times?"

"Who said I was cynical about relationships?"

"Okay, maybe not in so many words," Casey

said. "But come on. You're certainly skeptical about ours. Don't even try to deny it."

"I won't, no," Char said. "You're right. I am cynical, about us and in general. I mean, don't get me wrong. I believe in love. I believe in happily ever after. I'm just not sure it's in the cards for everyone."

Like her. She didn't have to say it. It was implied. "Is there anything I can do to change your mind about that?"

"Keep doing what you're doing. Slowly but surely, you're starting to change my mind."

"Glad to hear it." Casey rolled over onto his side and kissed her. "I intend to keep working at that."

"That's good. Enough serious talk, though. We don't have a lot of time left," Char said, as she ran her fingers down his torso.

It didn't take long for the blood to head in the same direction, making him hard again. It was a good thing he was young and didn't need much recovery time, because she had quite the appetite. Maybe it was true that women reached their sexual peak much later than men. If so, then they were probably perfect for each other. Casey didn't want to think anymore, as Char took the initiative and straddled him. No, he was content to lay back and enjoy it as she sheathed his engorged cock with a condom before positioning herself to take him inside her.

Casey put his hands on her hips, lifting himself up and into her. Even with next to no foreplay, he was able to enter her easily, and smoothly, and as Char arched her back and raised her hips to take him completely, Casey let out a moan. "That's it, baby. That feels so good," he said, as she began to move on top of him. It wouldn't be long before he surrendered all control and exploded inside her. It never took long. Yeah, he would miss this for sure. It might be the longest five days of Casey's life.

CHAPTER THIRTEEN

After seeing Casey off—with great reluctance—Char packed a few days worth of clothes and made the forty-five minute drive up to Canyon Lake. Fortunately, in typical Texas fashion, the weather changed again, with temperatures expected to be warm for the next several days. Perfect weather for being at the lake. If not for the long drive to work, and her preference to have some distance from her mother, Char wouldn't mind owning a house in Canyon Lake herself. Maybe she should look for a vacation retreat. Except that would entail taking an actual vacation, which is something Char hadn't done since she began working for the Generals, and didn't envision it happening anytime soon.

She arrived at the house shortly before noon, and her mother came out to greet her, Char's stepfather trailing close behind.

"You made it." Vicki Jennings gave Char an awkward hug as soon as she stepped out of the car. Then again, everything about their relationship tended toward awkward. It was only appropriate that the hug would be, too. Still, Char had to admit her mother looked good, sporting a natural tan and a new, shorter hairstyle. Retirement, remarriage, and life on the lake seemed to agree with her.

"Of course I made it. Did you think I wouldn't come?" Char asked. She extended a hand to her stepfather. "Hi, Scott."

"Char. It's nice to see you again. How was the drive?"

"In this car," she jerked her thumb back in the direction of the Mustang, "the drive's always fun."

"Then you should visit more often," Vicki said. "How long are you staying?"

"Through Monday." Char grabbed her bag from the back seat. "I'll probably drive back to town early Tuesday morning," she said. "I have to get back to work."

"You work too hard."

Char tried not to roll her eyes. If she'd said she was staying longer, her mother would think she wasn't working hard enough. That was the way things had always been. "Maybe I do, but I like my work. Besides, this is a busy time for us."

"Well, at least you're here for a few days," her stepfather said. "Weather's supposed to be nice. Maybe I can take you out on the boat later today or tomorrow, if you're interested."

She nodded. "I'd like that, yes." A boat ride over Christmas. Casey would be so jealous. It was most likely snowing where he was. Or at least frigid cold.

"We were about to eat lunch," Viki said. "It's nothing special, just chicken salad, but I'll get you a plate."

"That sounds great. Thank you." Char followed

them into the house, where she set down her bag in the guest room before going into the kitchen. She piled a hoagie roll high with chicken salad and grabbed some potato chips, then joined her mother and Scott out on the back deck.

Her mother poured her a glass of white wine, and Char took a sip as she looked out at the lake. No wonder her mother was more relaxed lately. The view was incredible. "It is gorgeous here."

"You're welcome anytime," Scott said. "Vicki and I were a little surprised you didn't drive up last night, since the hockey game was in the afternoon."

"I thought about it," Char admitted. Until she'd gotten a better offer. Walk on eggshells trying to avoid an argument with her mother, or have mind-blowing sex with Casey. It wasn't much of a choice. "But I ended up being invited to dinner at the team owner's house."

"Really?" Her mother's lips narrowed into what wasn't a frown, but wasn't a smile, either. "Do you have dinner at his house very often?"

Char shook her head. "No, it was the first time, and I wasn't the one he technically invited." She wasn't sure how much she should say, but after a second's hesitation, decided to just go for it. She couldn't spend three days with her mother without some prying into her private life, anyway. Might as well get it out of the way. "It was a dinner for the team, and I was invited by one of the players to attend as his guest."

"You mean like a date?"

"Yes." Char reached for a potato chip. "We've been seeing each other a little bit lately."

"Since when?" Vicki wanted to know. "And who is it?"

"Since a little more than a week ago. It's nothing serious, not so far, but he invited me to the dinner, so I went." Char shrugged her shoulders as if it were nothing. "And I'd rather not say who it is, until we have a better idea where things might be headed."

Her mother's expression changed again, and this time there was no mistaking the frown. "One of the players? Isn't that a bit of a conflict? And how old is he? I'm assuming he must be younger. I mean, I know there's that guy who plays for the team in Florida team who's in his forties, but isn't that kind of unusual?"

What was this? Twenty questions? Char took another drink of wine and forced a smile on her face. "No, it's not a conflict. Yes, he's a little bit younger." She kept her answer vague. "Yes, it's true that most of the players are. But I like him, and he likes me, and we have fun together. We're just going to take it day by day and see what happens." It was funny how her own perspective had changed over the course of the past week. Yep. Casey had definitely gotten to her.

Her stepfather gave her a genuine smile. "Then that's all that matters," he said, before turning to his wife. "Lay off the inquisition, Vicki. It's Christmas. Just let her be happy."

"Thank you, Scott." Char found herself grateful for her stepfather's calm and practical influence on her mother. Maybe Christmas wouldn't be so bad after all.

***

A light snow fell as Casey landed in Ottawa,

serving as a quick reminder that he wasn't in Texas anymore. It was good to be home, though, even if it was only for a few days.

His sister Cassie met him at baggage claim after he'd passed through customs. "Hey, little brother."

"Hi, Cass." He gave her a hug and kissed her cheek. "Thanks for coming to get me."

"Of course," she said. "I don't mind. How long are you here 'til? Wednesday, right?"

Casey nodded. "Yeah. We play the Sens here on Wednesday, so I got permission from coach to stay an extra day rather than travel back to Texas only to leave again," Casey said. His luggage came out on the conveyor, and he grabbed it, then walked with Cassie out to the parking lot.

"That works out good, then." They reached Cassie's car, and she unlocked the trunk for him to put his suitcase in. "It'll be nice to have you around, even if it's not for very long. Assuming we actually see you, that is."

"What's that supposed to mean?" Casey asked as he got in the car.

His sister laughed as she got in the driver's side. "As if you don't know? Most of the time when you're home, you're out carousing."

"Not always," Casey insisted, even though he knew she was right. Heck, he even had a couple of local girls he could always count on for no-strings hookups when he was home. Not anymore, though.

"Yeah, right." Cassie rolled her eyes. "I love you, Casey, but let's face it, you're a horndog of the worst kind."

"You mean I *was*. Past tense." He settled back

into his seat. "You're not going to believe this, but I'm changing, Cass. I met someone, and she's making me change my ways."

"And you're done with the tawdry one night stands? Well, I'll be damned." His sister turned her head to the side for a second. "Who is this girl, Casey? She must be something special."

"She's not a girl. She's a woman." He felt like it was an important distinction to make. "The most incredible woman I've ever met."

"Whoa. That's some high praise. Tell me more."

Casey wasn't even sure where to start. "She's kind and intelligent and classy," he said. "She's devoted her life to helping others. She's got a sense of humor, and we make each other laugh. She's a great cook. And she's smoking hot and great in bed."

Cassie let out a laugh. "The fact that that's the last thing you mentioned tells me this one probably *is* special. In fact, she sounds just about perfect, Casey."

"I don't know about perfect, but maybe perfect for me," he said, "and she's making me want be a better man."

"Nice," Cassie said. She stopped at a stoplight and turned to face him. "So when do we meet the woman who's making you forget all the ones before her?"

"I don't know. Probably not for a while." Casey doubted Char was anywhere near ready to take that step. He could live with that, as long as she eventually got there. "We're taking things kind of slow, at her request. It feels like the real deal, though. Or whatever the real deal should feel like." It wasn't as if he had a lot of previous experience, but this thing with Char... it felt pretty damn real to him.

***

Char was up before sunrise, drinking coffee out on the deck. Her mother and stepfather were still asleep, so she used the time to call Casey. Ottawa as an hour ahead, so she figured he'd be awake.

Sure enough, he answered on the first ring. "Hey, babe."

"Hi, sexy," she said. "Merry Christmas."

"Merry Christmas to you, too. How's the lake?"

"Gorgeous." She stretched her legs out. "I'm sitting here in my kimono, watching the sunrise over the water. It's breathtaking. I want you to see it sometime, Casey."

"I want to see it. In fact, I wish I could be there now. It's snowing here."

Char chuckled. "Of course it is. It's Canada in December." She stood up and walked down from the deck to the edge of the water. If the day turned out as nice as it looked like it would, she would definitely take Scott up on the offer of the boat ride. "I want to see where you're from, too, though."

"We can arrange that," he said. "My sister already wants to meet you."

"You told her about me?" Char dipped her foot into the edge of the water. A little cool, but not too bad.

"Is that okay?"

"Sure, it's fine. I told my mom about you," she said. "Not by name, though."

"You could've," Casey said. "I wouldn't mind."

"You're sure?" Char already knew the answer.

Casey seemed ready for more. She was the one trying to proceed with caution. Then again, she'd been burned before. He hadn't.

"Absolutely. I'm not embarrassed. I'm not holding back. I want to be with you, Char." The conviction carried through his voice.

"I want to be with you, too," she said. "I know I've been the one holding back a little, wanting to move slower. I'm working on catching up, though."

"You're doing fine, babe," Casey said. "We've got time. I'm not going anywhere."

Char smiled. "Then I'm not either," she said. "I'll see you in a few days, Casey."

"Yep. Until then, I'll miss you."

"Me too." Heck, who was she kidding? She already missed him.

CHAPTER FOURTEEN

C har survived an uneventful Christmas at the lake. The temperatures were perfect, and three of them went out on Scott's boat a couple of times. Her mother kept the prying into her personal life to a minimum, which was surprising considering Char dropped the bombshell that she'd been dating one of the players on the team. No arguments erupted, and overall, it was a pleasant three days. So much so that Char even considered staying an extra day. She had plenty of personal days saved up, and the team and majority of the staff wouldn't be back until Thursday.

However, she had plans to watch the game against the Senators with some of the girls at a local sports bar, so she stuck with the original plan and got up early Wednesday morning to make the drive back to town. With so many people still gone, the office was quiet, and Char got a lot of work done before leaving to watch the game.

It was an early Central time start, and by the time she arrived at the bar, most of the gang was already there, including Jessica, who enjoyed a rare weeknight off. Char was introduced to Kendall Myers, who dated the team's goalie, Beck Lawson, but missed a lot of functions and gatherings because she had two young children, one of whom had special needs. On this particular Wednesday, her kids were with their dad, allowing Kendall to join the others to watch the game.

All in all, it was a great group, and even though Char had worked with several of the women before on various Foundation projects and they weren't exactly strangers to her, she'd noticed a subtle shift since she and Casey had gone public with the fact they were seeing each other. Now, Char wasn't just the one who organized various projects and brought the group together. She was part of the group. And she liked it.

"I ordered the first round of drinks already," Angie said, "but I'll wave our guy back here to get your order."

"That's fine," Char said. "The next round is on me."

"No one's going to argue with that," Maya said. "I'm way too tense about this game."

"Join the club. Trevor's always nervous playing back in Ottawa," Dani Greer said, and it made sense. Trevor had begun his NHL career with the Senators.

"Casey loves it, because it's his hometown," Char told them. "When I talked to him this morning, he was pretty pumped to be playing in front of his family and friends."

"Good. Hopefully you're still his good luck charm." Jessica gave Char a wink.

"Let's hope so," she said, and they settled in to watch the game. It wasn't the same as being in the arena, with the boisterous home crowd, but watching the game on TV with a group of friends beat watching it alone. When Casey scored a power play goal midway through the first period to open the scoring, they cheered and high-fived each other.

As the game announcers talked about Casey's recent scoring streak, even proclaiming him to be the hottest player in the NHL right now, Maya turned to Char. "Okay, it's settled. This thing between you and Casey needs to continue being a thing."

Char laughed. "All right. I'll see what I can do." The truth was, she wanted it to continue being a thing, too. For a long time.

***

Casey scored the first goal, and notched an assist on another as the Generals went on to a 4-2 victory over Ottawa. This time the holster was awarded to Colton for his two goals, but that was fine with Casey. Heck, he wished there were more of them to go around. This was a true team in every sense of the word, and after some early season struggles, they were kicking on all cylinders.

"One, two, three, team," they shouted in the locker room as they ended the post-game speeches and dispersed for the showers. Casey never tried to establish himself as a leader on the team before. He preferred to just have fun, live it up. Sure, he stepped in line to help out when needed, but he'd always been a follower, not a leader. And he'd been okay with that. Lately, though, he'd been more vocal in the locker room. It probably coincided with his scoring streak. Since he'd led the team in scoring over the past five games, he began to see himself take on more of a leadership role. He may never wear a "C" or an "A" on his sweater, because Colton, Alex and Ryder were firmly entrenched as the team's captain and alternate captains, but he could still be a leader. Somehow. Maybe it was Char's influence, but Casey thought maybe his own charity might be the way to make his mark.

When he met up with his family after the game, he pitched the idea. "I need something, a cause for me, and I can promote it at the games. Like some guys support cancer research, paraplegics, diabetes. I don't know what mine is, yet, but I'm working on finding it out. I can sponsor suites at the games, so people who wouldn't otherwise get the opportunity can go to a Generals game," he said. "I'd have to base it San Antonio, but maybe I can do something here, too." After all, Ottawa was home.

"I'm proud of you, Casey," his mother said, and his father echoed the sentiment,

"Yep," Cassie said. "It's like my baby brother's growing up right before my eyes."

Casey turned to her and grinned. "Maybe I am. That's what it feels like. You'll still be my best girl, though." He held up his phone and snapped a picture of the two of them, his arm around her.

"Perfect," he said, then posted the photo to his Instragram account.

***

Char wanted to call Casey after the game, but she was out with her friends and assumed he might be going out to celebrate with his family, so she opted for sending a him text, congratulating him on both the win, and adding to his scoring total.

He responded right away, a short message that said, *Thanks, babe. See ya soon. Save a kiss for me.*

A kiss? She replied. *You earned a lot more than a kiss, and I can't wait to deliver.*

She slept restlessly that night, missing Casey and thinking about ways they could make up for the time apart. It might have only been five days, but it felt like a lot longer. "Yeah, Char, you've got it bad," she said to herself as she drove to work, knowing full well she probably wouldn't be able to concentrate, wondering when the team's plane would arrive back in town.

The mood at team headquarters was jubilant after the win, which moved San Antonio into a tie for the final playoff spot. Most acknowledged it was too soon to talk playoffs, though, and were more focused on the upcoming All-Star Game. With the game being played in San Antonio, the home team was all but certain to have at least three players selected. It looked more and more like Casey would be one of them.

Char was at her desk drinking her morning coffee and catching up on email when Leah gave a knock at her door before walking in. "What's up?" she asked.

"Nothing. I just wanted to see how you were?"

Char gave her assistant a puzzled look. "I'm fine. Why wouldn't I be?"

"I don't know. I just wondered..." Leah looked at the floor.

"Wondered what, Leah? Can you please get to the point?"

"Okay. It might not be my place, but I think there's something you should see," she said. "If it was me, I think I'd want to know."

Char frowned. "What are you talking about?" So far, Leah wasn't making a lot of sense, but she sensed it wasn't good.

"Well... you've sort of been seeing Casey Denault, right? I mean, you haven't said anything to anyone here, but people like to talk."

"Yes, they do." Even if she and Casey hadn't made a public announcement, they hadn't denied anything, or tried to hide anything, either. "And yes, I have. Why?"

"Do you follow him on Instagram?"

"No." Char shook her head. "I've never gotten into the whole Instagram thing." Maybe it was time she did, but she found it hard enough to keep with Twitter and Facebook. Besides, Leah and others on the staff were younger and more social media savvy than her. She'd been content to leave Instagram to them.

"Then you haven't seen this. And you should."

"See what?" Judging from the way Leah acted, Char guessed she wouldn't like it.

"Casey's Instagram account. He posted this last night." Leah handed Char her cell phone, which was opened to Instagram, and the latest photo on what was, presumably, Casey's account.

The picture looked like a selfie, one Casey had taken of himself with his arm around a young blonde woman, He had a big grin on his face, and the caption read, *Always happy to be back in Ottawa with my best girl.*

CHAPTER FIFTEEN

C har stared at the phone display, not wanting to believe the image she was seeing in front of her. If there was a way to unsee it, she wanted to find it. That wasn't possible, though. It was there, plain as day, Casey and the beautiful blonde. The *young*, beautiful blonde. She couldn't forget the young part.

Her chest tightened. So this was Casey's best girl, huh? What about her? Or all of the dozens of others before her? Was this one special, like Char believed she might be, or was she being played for a fool, too?

It was hard to know what to feel toward the woman in the picture. Jealousy? Anger? Char hadn't wasted energy on those emotions for Graham's mistress, and then been married three years when she found out. No, her only anger was reserved for her unfaithful husband, and didn't even last long, instead being replaced by emptiness. An emptiness which, if Char was honest with herself, hadn't disappeared until recently. Until Casey. And now...

As tears welled in her eyes, Char tried to blink

them away. She passed the phone back to her assistant. "You can go now, Leah, and take this with you."

Leah took the phone from her. "I'm sorry. I just thought.."

"Yes, I get it. You thought I should know," Char said. "And you were probably right. I don't blame you. I would, however, like you to leave now." The words came out harsher than she intended. Char didn't want to shoot the messenger. She just wanted to be left alone before she broke down.

"Yes. Of course. I'll go," her assistant said, but stopped and turned when she got to the door. "I really am sorry," she added, before showing herself out.

Yeah. That makes two of us.

Alone, Char sank down in her chair. She should be embarrassed. Check that. She *was* embarrassed. She'd confused a few nights of great sex with something more, and then, because it all felt do damn good, she forgot about caution and discretion and whatever else, and she put herself out there. She'd worn his freaking jersey to the game, knowing it made a statement. Then she'd taken it a step further, letting him come to her office to pick her up. Heck, she even accompanied Casey to dinner at Mr. Johnson's house. They might've skipped Facebook official, but who needed that when Char was showing up at the boss's house on Casey's arm?

All for him to play her for the fool?

No. There had to be some explanation, right?

Char tapped at her mouse to wake up her computer, then navigated her web browser to Instagram. She didn't have an account, and didn't plan on getting one anytime soon. It didn't matter, though.

She didn't need one to view Casey's account. She'd seen the user name on Leah's phone. cdenualt19sa.

There it was.

And there *she* was. Casey's new 'best girl.'

Char scrolled through the pictures posted to the account, searching for more clues. There were no pictures of her with Casey. Had they ever taken any? She couldn't recall any. Not even at the amusement park, when they were on the roller coaster. At the time, she'd chalked it up to adrenaline, or wanting to respect her privacy, or... something.

Who was she fooling? Nobody, really.

As she scrolled through the rest of the pictures on Casey's page, Char found a lot of them were hockey related, like the one of him wearing the toy holster, after earning player of the game honors. There were pictures of some of the other guys. Further back, there was one of Casey with an older couple, whom Char figured might be his parents. And right before that, there was another of the blonde girl. Great. She'd been around for a while.

Char's phone beeped, and she glanced at the screen. It was a text from Casey.

Just landed. Ready to collect that kiss. Where are u?

She'd almost forgotten about the flirtatious text she sent the night before, but now it all came back to her. Was Casey's plan just to step right back into what they had going before the holiday? What about his so-called 'best girl?'

At work, Char replied. Where else did he think she'd be?

I'll come by.

Char thought for a minute. She didn't want him coming to the office. Not now, since Leah and who knew who else had seen the Instagram photo. *No. I'll meet you somewhere. The burger place down the street?*

Great. See you soon, babe. I have a kiss for you, too. ;)

Char set her phone down. She couldn't muster a suggestive or flirtatious reply. Not now. She'd meet him, though, and get it over with. Who knows. Maybe he'd even have a good explanation. Somehow, she doubted it, but she'd listen. Char felt as if she owed Casey that much.

***

Even when the team's mood was upbeat after a victory, Casey found the charter flights back home to be long and boring, and this one was no exception. Nothing seemed to make the time pass any faster.

Some of the guys played a card game. Others napped, or played games on their phones or tablets. Noah read a comic book, even lent one to Casey. Casey tried to read it, but couldn't concentrate. All he could think about was how badly he wanted to see Char. *Needed* to see her. Five days was way too long, especially after the message she'd sent last night.

He sent her a text as soon as they landed, intending to go to her office. Instead, she replied and suggested meeting at a burger place. That was fine. It was lunch time. As long as they had privacy to talk, because Casey had a lot on his mind.

Casey arrived before she did, and got a table,

where he sipped a soda while he waited, running through what he wanted to say in his head. When Char finally did walk in, the sight of her nearly took his breath away. God, how he'd missed her.

"You're sure a sight for sore eyes," Casey said, jumping up to kiss her. He took her in his arms, not caring that they were in a public place. The only thing he cared about was that he wanted to kiss her, touch her, taste her, much like he had that night at the club. Her birthday. The night they'd started this thing that he now couldn't imagine ever wanting to stop.

Char responded to the kiss, but for only a second before pulling away, and when she did, her expression was cold. "I let my guard down for a minute, and you got your kiss. Don't bet on getting any more, though."

What the hell? The words were so unexpected, they sent Casey's mind reeling. "What are you talking about? Is something wrong?" Who was he kidding? Something was very wrong. He just couldn't figure out what.

"Actually, yes. I'm little upset right now." Char pulled out a chair and sat down, then took her phone out of her purse. She tapped at the screen for a second, then passed it to him. "It's this. I'm hoping you can explain this to me. See, I thought we had a pretty good thing going on here, but it looks like I'm wrong. It seems this girl is your new 'best girl' and I don't see any way I can compete with that, right? I mean, she's younger and prettier, and—" Char stopped as her voice cracked, then blinked hard, as if trying to keep from crying. "Tell me I'm wrong, Casey. Can you do that?"

CHAPTER SIXTEEN

Casey's brain struggled to catch up, and make some sense out of this. Sometime between yesterday afternoon, when he last talked to Char, or heck, last night, when they exchanged a couple of fun, flirtatious, text messages, and today, something changed, and not for the better. Now she was crying. Okay, maybe not outright tears, but she was at least on the verge of tears. And worst of all, she accused him of cheating on her. What the hell?

"I don't even know what you're talking about, but whatever you think it is—Yes, you're wrong." Casey could promise that much. He never cheated on her, and sure as hell as didn't plan to. He grabbed the phone from Char' hand, since it seemed to be the source of the problem. One look at the screen, and he knew why.

Son of a bitch! How could he have been so careless, so incredibly stupid? His manager, his family, heck even some of his teammates had warned him to be smarter about what he posted on social media, because it could come back to haunt him. Casey knew that, but still didn't expect this.

"Well?" Char demanded. "Do you have an explanation?"

"Yes. I'm an idiot," Casey said. He saw no point in trying to sugar coat it.

"I'm inclined to agree with that," Char said. "I thought you were smarter, but I don't have a lot of room to talk, because clearly, I'm an idiot, too. I am curious what you think your mistake was? Cheating, or getting caught?" Her tone was ice, leaving no doubt in Casey's mind that if he ever did, in fact, cheat on her, she'd make damn sure he paid for it, and dearly. At least in this case, he was completely innocent, albeit stupid.

"Neither," he said, "Because it's not what you think. I know I'm not the first guy to ever say that to a woman, but in this case, it's true. I admit it looks bad, though, and I can see how someone might get the wrong impression." Especially since he had a terrible reputation. That sure didn't do him any favors. Yeah, he'd earned this one. First, by being a self-avowed playboy, and then, even as he tried to move away from that lifestyle, by being careless with what he posted on social media.

"It's not what I think? Okay, then, what is it?" At least she sat down, calmly, and wasn't ranting. Or worse, storming out of the restaurant without giving him the chance to explain. No, even when she was hurting—and Casey could see that she was—Char had too much class to cause a scene.

All the more reason to love her.

"My so-called 'best girl,' the one in the picture, is my sister, Cassandra," he explained. "Cassie for short. She's older than me, by all of ten months." He let out a laugh. "I guess our parents were in a hurry to get back in the saddle after she was born. Anyway, our birthdays even worked out so that we were in the same grade in school, and most people always assumed we were twins," he said. "The similar names probably added to that misconception."

"Cassie and Casey. Cute." Char didn't sound like she meant it, and Casey wondered if she wasn't quite believing him. If he was on the other side, would he believe him?

"We've always been close," he said. "I jokingly call her my best girl, because I've always said no one else will ever hold the same place in my heart as my sister. Up until a couple of weeks ago, that was the truth. So many women, but none of them ever meant anything to me. Then you came along, and completely gobsmacked me."

"Gobsmacked? I didn't even know anyone ever used that word." She laughed, so maybe that was a good sign.

"They must, because I just did," Casey said.

"Your sister, huh? She's the one in the picture?"

Casey nodded. "Yeah, we took it after the game last night. We were out celebrating the win," he said. "You believe me, right?"

"I'm working on it. I want to." Still, she sounded dubious.

"Here, I'll prove it. I'll get her on the phone." Casey pulled his phone out of his pocket, tapping at the screen.

"You don't have to do that."

Casey held up a hand. "Yes. I do. I want this settled."

Fortunately, Cassie answered right away, and her face appeared in the Facetime display. "Hey, little brother. I wasn't expecting to hear from you. What's up?"

"Not much," he said. "I just got back to Texas. Anyway, there's someone here who wants to say hi to you."

"Is it the girl? The one you didn't stop talking about the whole time you were home?" The amusement was evident in Cassie's voice. "Put her on."

"Just a sec," Casey said, then passed the phone to Char. Surely she'd see Cassie's face on the display, and everything would be fine. It had to be.

"So you're the famous Cassie," Casey heard Char say when she took the phone from him.

"Yep. And we're not even twins, believe it or not."

"That's what he said. Anyway, I'm Char and this is really strange, but whatever. Is it true that he talked about me all weekend?"

"Yep, he sure did." Cassie's voice sounded muffled, but Casey could hear enough. Enough to know he was being embarrassed, but also enough to know that Char would have to believe him now. And that was the only thing that mattered. "So when are you coming to Ottawa so we can all meet you? Because the whole family is anxious to meet the woman who's finally succeeded in taming my brother."

***

The woman's face on the phone display matched the one on the Instagram post, and it would be pretty hard to fake something like this. Besides, now that Char had the chance to look at Casey's face across the table from her, and Cassie's on Facetime, the family resemblance was evident. Char hated that she'd jumped to conclusions and not trusted him.

"I don't know," she said. "Maybe I'll get there sometime. I'd like to meet you, too." Was that where this was headed? They chatted for another minute, then Char said goodbye to Cassie and passed the phone back to Casey.

He took it from her, then walked a few steps away from the table to finish the conversation, then returned. "Well?" he asked. "Do I get to live another day?"

"Yes," Char said. "I'm sorry. I jumped to the wrong conclusion. I saw you, with your arm around some other woman—"

"Yeah, and I called her my best girl." Casey raked a hand through his hair. "People are always telling me to be smarter about social media, and this proves that I have to be. That was dumb. Careless. Reckless. Maybe it was cute when we were teenagers, but not now. Not when I'm in the public eye. And especially not when I'm dating an incredible woman like you."

"Uh huh." Char managed a smile. "How about you rethink who you call your 'best girl' from now on, okay? Or better yet, call me your only girl."

"I like that better, because you *are* the only one." Casey exhaled audibly. "Does that mean you believe me?"

"Yes, I do." Char didn't even hesitate before answering. The family resemblance, and the earnestness in Casey's voice and expression couldn't be faked. He might have the reputation as a playboy, but in many ways, he was still a kid. Immature at times, but adorably sweet, too. "I never wanted to think the worst of you, Casey," she said. "My assistant showed me the picture. I'm not even on Instagram." And now, she was less sure she wanted to be.

"Ah, the assistant, trying to stir up shit," Casey said, making Char laugh.

"It's okay. Leah means well. My staff is very protective of me," Char said. "They know I don't date a lot, and then you came into the picture..."

"I get it. They think they have to protect you from wolves like me."

Char cocked her to the side. "Well, don't they?" She might be teasing, but the question was serious at the same time. Would Casey brush it off, or would he give her a serious response? It would tell her a lot about where things stood, and where they were going.

"A few weeks ago, they would've been wise to warn you about me," he said. "I was the guy every woman should've been warned about. I've been a jerk. Sure, I treat women right when I'm with them. At least I like to think I do." Char gave a slight nod of her head, because it was true. It may have started as a one-night stand, but he'd been so very considerate of her that night. Yes, he was horny and wanted his release, but he'd shown more interest in satisfying her desires first. And one thing was for sure. Casey Denault knew how to pleasure a woman.

"Then you came along," he said. "And suddenly I was—"

"Gobsmacked?" she supplied with a smirk.

"Exactly. See it's a good word." Casey smiled. "I didn't know what hit me. I still don't. I just know you make me want to be a better man," he said. "You make me want to be faithful, committed, all of that, because I know if I stray, it's over, and I won't see you again... and that's a day I don't want to face."

"Me neither," Char said. "Like you said, I think I'm better with you, too, Casey. I'm more relaxed. I'm more fun. I know I'm happier, and enjoy life more." That was the biggest thing. He made her happy. "I didn't want to believe that Instragram post, because I don't want this to end."

"It's not ending," Casey said. "Not if I can help it. As far as I'm concerned, it's just beginning."

As Char listened to his words, she realized it was what she wanted too. Not the end, but rather only the beginning. A future of limitless possibilities. "I want that," she said. "I may be insecure at times, and have my doubts about some things, but I want to be with you, Casey. I want to see where this road leads next."

"Then I'll show you." He reached across the table for her hand, then brought it to his lips and kissed it. "And I promise it'll be a hell of a ride."

Char nodded. "I believe you, and I can't wait to see where this ride takes me next." She choked back a laugh. "Let's just not make it as scary as the Iron Rattler, okay?"

CHAPTER SEVENTEEN

San Antonio went 6-3-2 over its next eleven games, leaving the team in playoff position heading into the All-Star break. Usually, that meant a few days of rest for Casey, but not this year. No, this year he'd be playing in the All-Star game. Casey was still in awe. Not only did he earn his fist All-Star selection, but he'd be playing in front of the hometown fans. Not just the Generals' home fans, though, but one very special woman, too.

Talk about changing Casey's life, and for the better. With Char's help and guidance, he'd put the steps in motion to begin the Casey's Kids program, benefitting juvenile diabetes. Each week, he'd invite local kids who suffered from juvenile diabetes to attend a Generals home game in a luxury box Casey paid for.

He knew he'd take a financial hit in renting the box, at least in the beginning, but in the long-term, it would be worth it. Awareness, and money raised for a worthy cause. Char taught him to think ahead. It wasn't just about tonight, the next girl, whatever felt good. Stardom came quickly for Casey, and probably too easily, as well. He'd never paid his dues. He was twenty-four years old, and a millionaire, and women wanted him. Lots of women? What else mattered?

Now, it all did. His reputation mattered. Char mattered. He wanted to be a leader. A role model. Someone who could be counted on. Looked up to. He was an all-star now. He had a future to think about, too, and Casey knew who he wanted to share it with.

The Western conference All-Stars gathered in the Generals' home locker room before taking the ice for the skills competition. In the visitor's locker room, the Eastern conference All-Stars were probably going through similar rituals and preparations. Casey knew the home crowd would be on the side of Western conference, and especially himself, and his two Generals teammates, defenseman Noah Mann, and their goalie, Becker Lawson.

Casey would be competing in the fastest skater competition, as well as the one-timer shooting competition, both of which played to his strengths. Even better, he was sharing a locker room with players he'd looked to over the years, and considered among the best in the NHL. Now, instead of rivals, they were teammates. Yeah, he could get used to this All-Star thing.

Since the Generals' captain wasn't participating in the game, the Western Conference needed a captain for the weekend, and after a vote, the other guys bestowed the honor on Casey. He tried to think about what Colton would do, and how he would lead. Colton had endured his troubles, too, but he'd grown up and turned into not only a great player, but a great captain and role model as well. "One, two, three, All-Star!" Casey shouted as he prepared to lead them out on the ice. "Let's do this."

He heard the cheers as he took the ice, and looked to the crowd, searching for his girl. It didn't take long for Casey to spot Char, and he raised a hand and blew her a kiss. She was there. For him. The future seemed brighter than it had ever been.

***

The crowd cheered for all of the players, but the loudest cheers were reserved for the three Generals All-Stars, first Noah, them Becker, and finally Casey, who would be serving as captain. Char was happy to lead the way in cheering when his name was announced.

"Look at that, he's blowing you a kiss," Beck's girlfriend, Kendall, observed.

Sure enough, it looked as if Casey was, indeed, blowing her a kiss. Char liked it. She liked the man he'd become.

"That's sweet." The observation came from a young woman Char hadn't met before, but accompanied Kendall to the game. She was introduced as Kendall's daughter's doctor. Riley, or something like that.

Char gave her a smile. "Yes. Casey's a sweetheart."

"Noah's sweet, too," Kendall said, and Char figured out what was happening. Kendall hoped to set Riley up on a date with Noah.

There was a time when Char would've steered well clear of that conversation. Now, she felt herself itching to chime in. She knew this team, these players. All of them. And she could speak to their character.

"Yes, and he's a lot of fun." Known for his playful personality and tendency to joke around, Char couldn't wait to see what Noah planned to entertain the crowd tonight. "I'm going to be working with him on a new charity golf tournament."

"That's nice," the young doctor said. "He's a good guy, then?"

"He sure is. They're all good guys," Char said. "I got the best, though."

"Yeah, of course you'd say that." Kendall rolled her eyes. "Good thing you're not biased or anything."

"Nope. I don't think he's the best. I know he is." Char leaned back in her seat, excited to watch Casey compete tonight, and for the rest of their adventure together.

###

Keep reading for a preview of *Breaking the Ice*, book 7 in the Men of the Ice series, available October, 2016.

BREAKING THE ICE

Chapter One

The NHL All-Star game. It wasn't the Stanley Cup, and some of the guys who were used to being selected to the game year after year, probably didn't get excited about it anymore, but Noah Mann considered it an honor to be participating. It would be his first All-Star game, and it would be played in front of the hometown fans in San Antonio. Because San Antonio was the host city, there were more Generals players selected to the game than there would be if it were played in any other NHL city. After all, the league wanted to play to the home crowd and give them something to cheer for.

Noah was well aware that this played a factor in his selection, but he didn't really care. For a kid from Red Deer, Alberta who'd been drafted in the fifth round and toiled in relative obscurity in the American Hockey League affiliate in Iowa for years before finally earning a shot in the NHL—thank you, expansion draft— playing in the All-Star game wasn't something that happened every year. Noah planned to enjoy it.

He especially planned to enjoy the skills

competition, which would allow him to show off his powerful shot in the hardest shot competition, and have a little fun in the Breakaway Challenge. He might not win either one, but that didn't matter to Noah nearly as much as having a good time. Sure, his more serious teammates sometimes razzed him about being too much of a practical joker, but Noah knew it was only teasing. He'd proven, time and again, that he took hockey seriously, especially when it came to giving his all to his team and his community. But Noah also lived by the motto that life was too short to be serious all the time.

The actual All-Star game would be the following afternoon, and Noah would take that seriously. Tonight, though, his primary objective was to have fun and entertain the fans.

"What do you have planned tonight?" Noah's teammate, Generals goalkeeper Becker Lawson, asked him in the locker room before they got ready to take the ice. "Anything special?"

Noah shrugged. "Maybe, but I'm not going to tell you. I want it to be a secret until I unveil it to the crowd."

Beck gave him a puzzled look. "Huh?" Then it apparently dawned on him. "Oh. You mean for the challenge. You must have some gag planned."

Noah didn't care for the term gag, but he didn't object to it, either. "What'd you think I meant?"

"Never mind," Beck said. "I was talking about after the game, or rather the competition. Do you have any plans?"

"Oh, that." Talk about being on opposite pages. Noah shook his head. "Nah. I'll probably just go home.

Make it a quiet night." Noah was single, which wasn't always easy on a team where it seemed like a lot of the guys were settling down, or at least pairing up. Heck, even the Generals' most notorious playboy, Casey Denault, had turned into a one-woman man in recent months, after finding love with the director of the team's charity foundation.

Charlene Simmons might be sixteen years older than Casey, but for some reason, they seemed to fit together, and all the guys were hoping it would work out. For one thing, Casey's scoring streak since getting together with Char had resulted in quite a winning streak for the Generals. Noah sure wouldn't complain about that, even if he did wonder if the world had suddenly gone mad. Casey, monogamous? If not mad, something close to it.

"Why? Are you going out?" Noah asked Beck. He assumed the goaltender would have plans with his girlfriend.

His teammate nodded. "Yeah. That's why I ask. Kendall's hoping you'll join us for a late dinner."

"As a third wheel?" Yeah. The world had gone mad. "Sorry, not my gig."

"Yep, that's what I told Kendall," Beck said dryly. "Don't shoot the messenger, but she's got something else in mind. Like a blind date."

"A blind date?" Noah was shaking his head before the words were even out, and when they were out, they weren't no. Instead, he asked, "With who?"

"One of Ali's doctors," Beck said. "Her name is Riley."

Beck's girlfriend's daughter suffered from a condition called Rett Syndrome, which Noah didn't know much about, other than she couldn't walk on her own and had seizures, and apparently had a doctor that Kendall thought he needed to meet. "Kendall wants to set me up with her daughter's doctor?"

"Yep. She's a pediatric neurology resident," Beck said. "And she's pretty hot."

"Not the most important criteria," Noah muttered. Still, he had to admit it didn't hurt.

"I didn't say it was," Beck countered. He reached for his mask. "Anyway, she's here tonight. Sitting with Kendall and Char. Have a look. Give it some thought. No pressure, though."

No pressure? Right. Noah already felt as if he had no choice but to accept. The woman was here. He'd look like an ass if he didn't even want to so much as meet her. Gee, thanks, Beck.

***

It was her first full day off in more than two weeks, and Dr. Riley Marks had intended to spend it sleeping. Sleep, was an increasingly precious commodity for a second-year medical resident, and when Riley clocked out after her last shift, the only date she had interest in was one with her pillow. Kendall Myers had other ideas, which explained—sort of—why Riley found herself sitting in the stands of a hockey arena, along with Kendall and a woman she'd never met before, but also apparently dated a player from the San Antonio Generals, preparing to watch the NHL All-Star Skills Competition.

"I'd rather be in my bed," Riley muttered, sipping Diet Mountain Dew through a straw in the hopes that she'd stay awake. She was used to running on adrenaline, anyway.

"No, you wouldn't," Kendall said. "Sleep is overrated, and this will be fun. I've been trying to get you to come to a game all season."

It was true. Ever since Kendall had met Becker Lawson the previous summer when he coached her son in the Generals youth hockey cap, she'd become a huge fan of all things hockey. And ever since Riley had joined the medical team providing care to Kendall's daughter Alison, Kendall had started on a mission to try to turn Riley into a fan, too. Her reasoning was that Riley needed to occasionally relax and have fun, something Riley didn't disagree with. The problem was she didn't have time.

This afternoon, when Kendall's phone call woke Riley from her sleep, she'd reluctantly agreed to tag along. Maybe by accepting, Kendall would stop asking. And maybe it would take Riley's mind off of work for a little while.

"Besides, I want you to see Noah," Kendall continued. "I really think he'd be perfect for you."

"Whoa, wait a minute, what?" Maybe it was the lack of sleep interfering with her cognitive speed, but it took Riley a second to catch up to what Kendall was saying. "You're trying to set me up on a date? With a hockey player?" She shook her head. "No. That's all sorts of inappropriate."

"Why?" Kendall countered.

"Um, because your daughter is my patient."

"Right… which would be a problem if I was suggesting that *we* go on a date. As in you and me," Kendall said, circling her finger from Riley back to herself. "Which is not happening, for a number of obvious reasons. Did you miss the part where I said it was Noah I wanted you meet? Noah, a hockey player who has absolutely zero connection to your work?"

"No." Riley sighed. "Okay, maybe inappropriate was the wrong word. It's still a bad idea."

"Why are you so opposed?"

"Because I've told you. Repeatedly. I don't have time."

"Yes, and if every busy professional constantly used that as an excuse, no one would ever date or get married, and the population would eventually die off."

Riley rolled her eyes. "Melodramatic much?"

"Fine. I won't say another word," Kendall promised. "Just sit and watch, and when it's all over, if you haven't had a good time, if you aren't even a little bit interested, we can forget we ever had this conversation."

It sounded like a good enough deal to Riley, so she settled back into her seat. She'd try to relax, try to have fun. She wasn't being fixed up with any hockey player, though. No way, no how.

She sat through the introduction of the Eastern Conference All-Stars, none of whom Riley knew anything about. It wasn't like she'd ever watched a hockey game before in her life. Then it was time to introduce the All-Stars from the Western Conference, ending with the players representing the home team. Becker first, followed by some guy named Casey Denault, who was dating the other woman who'd accompanied them to the game.

"At defense, from your hometown San Antonio Generals, number forty-seven, Noah Mann!" At the announcement, the crowd let out a loud cheer, and Riley leaned forward in her seat, trying to get a closer look at the guy Kendall seemed to think was perfect for her. He skated to the center of the ice, waved to each side of the arena, then went to join the other players where they all stood.

"So what do you think?" Kendall wanted to know.

"I don't know… it's a little hard to tell from this far away," Riley said. "I suppose he's kind of cute."

"He's a really nice, guy, too," Casey's girlfriend said. "I'm actually working with him to start up a new charity golf event."

Riley nodded. "That is nice." So he was cute, and believed in doing things for charity. That didn't mean she was going on a date with him.

The competition began with the fastest skater, which Casey participated in, but didn't win, then it was time for the Breakaway Challenge, in which players took one-on-one breakaway shots at the goal. Instead of just shooting the puck, though, they also tried to entertain the crowd. That seemed to play to Noah's strength, as in his first attempt, he fired a beach ball at the goal instead of the puck.

"He did that move last summer in camp," Kendall said. "The kids all loved it."

"I'm sure," Riley said absently. Okay, it was kind of clever, but she wasn't won over.

On his second attempt, Noah donned a super hero cape, and Riley's interest was piqued. Was it? No. Surely not. She peered closer. It was.

"Who is he dressed as?" Kendall asked. "I know it's not Superman. The color is wrong."

"It's Hyperion," Riley said.

Kendall frowned. "I've never heard of him, and I have a ten-year-old. I feel like a failure as a mother."

Riley laughed. "Relax. Plenty of people don't know Hyperion." She did, because she knew her super heroes. And so, apparently, did Noah, which meant Riley was officially intrigued.

"Okay, you win," she told Kendall. "I'd like to meet this guy after all."

***

The Breakaway Challenge was less about hockey shots than it was about entertaining the crowd, and Noah did his best to oblige. For some of the guys, that meant trick shots, for others it mean costumes and disguises. Noah tried a little bit of both. The beach ball shot was an old favorite, but he knew he could do better, and that was why he brought out the superhero for his next attempt. Not just any superhero, though. No, he went with Hyperion, whom he figured half the audience didn't know. There was a reason for the choice, though, and it garnered big applause. He opted for a basic spin-o-rama move for his last attempt, and hoped it was enough, and that the hometown crowd would vote him to victory.

Sure enough, when all the fan votes were in, Noah was declared the winner of the Breakaway Challenge. It meant a point for the Western Conference, but more importantly, he won a new car. He didn't need a car, but Noah was glad to win it. He had big plans for that car, and when he was interviewed by the television crew after the presentation, he let the fans know.

Even though he wasn't a fan of public speaking, Noah was happy to take the microphone for this. "First I want to say thanks to the all the fans here in the arena, and those watching at home, for voting for me, and thanks to our sponsors for the new car, which I will be donating to the youth center here in San Antonio. I've had a chance to visit before, and see firsthand the work they do, and it's something I believe a lot in and want to support," he said. "Besides, they need a new car a lot more than I do."

The last line earned laughter from the fans, and plenty of applause. As Noah finished the interview, he tried to glance into the rows of spectators to see where Kendall was sitting with the mystery woman he was supposed to meet, but there were too many people and too many cameras. So much for that. He'd have to find out what she looked like when he met for the first time, assuming he agreed to go. He hadn't committed himself to anything yet.

Noah also competed in the hardest shot competition, which he knew going into that he wouldn't win. He liked to believe his shot was hard, and knew plenty of goalies hated to face it, but it wasn't anywhere close to setting any records. No, his big moment of glory, such that it was, was getting that car for the shelter.

The Western Conference won the competition, and Noah was glad to have contributed. He got plenty of props from the other guys, especially those on his team, for gifting the car to charity.

"Congrats, man," Beck said when they were back in the locker room afterward. "You won her over and she hasn't even met you yet."

Noah frowned. "Won who over?"

"Riley. C'mon, don't tell me you forget. I just got a text from Kendall. Must've been the whole charity thing, but Riley's anxious to meet you." Beck said. "So hurry up and get changed."

"I didn't do it to impress the girl," Noah grumbled as he headed off to the shower. "I didn't agree to go out with her, either." It wasn't looking like he had much choice in the matter, though.

Fifteen minutes later, he stood in front of the mirror combing his hair while Beck tried to hurry him along. "Kendall's waiting outside with Riley. You're pretty enough, let's go."

"Bite me." Noah shot him a glare, but set the comb back in his locker and put his watch on. "I hate blind dates." He'd been on two before, and both had been disasters. If this one turned out the same, Noah would make sure Beck didn't forget it.

"Yeah, but look at the bright side. You'll be with Kendall and me," Beck said. "So if it's not working out, we'll know, and we'll just call it a night."

"That might be the one saving grace." Noah left with the locker room with Beck and they went out the players entrance. A few yards away, he saw Kendall waiting, along with a petite blonde. Was that the famous Riley? If so, she was, quite possibly, the most beautiful woman Noah had ever seen. "That's the doctor?"

Beck chuckled. "Sure is. Bet you're glad you agreed to this now."

Books by Michele Shriver

Women's Fiction:

After Ten
Tears and Laughter
Aggravated Circumstances

Contemporary Romance:

Finding Forever
Leap of Faith
The Art of Love
Starting Over
Love & Light
Dissonance
Healing Hearts (winter 2016)
Fade into Love (spring 2017)

The Men of the Ice Novellas:

Playing for Keeps
Crossing the Line
Winning it All
Scoring at Love
Chasing the Prize
Making an Impact
Breaking the Ice (2016)
Going all In (2017)
Beating the Odds (2017)

Boxed Sets:

Heroes to Swoon For
Spring into Love
Score One For Love
Christmas Pets and Kisses
Spring into Romance
Love Notes
First Glance
Christmas Pets and Kisses 2

Thank you for reading. I hope you enjoyed the story and will consider posting an honest review of this book on the site you purchased it from.

If you purchased this book prior to October 31, 2016, please visit: http://bit.ly/1U1T4iD to enter to win an autographed San Antonio Generals jersey.

Receive a free digital download of the San Antonio Generals program by subscribing to Michele Shriver's newsletter: http://eepurl.com/323sj

Author's Note and Acknowledgements

I hope you enjoyed Casey and Char's story, because it sure was fun to write. As an author, I never know why it is that some books are easier than others. They just are. While book five in this series was a struggle, even making me second guess the decision to extend the series, this one flowed right from the opening sentence and never gave me the fits that the previous did. It's books like this that make me love the job of being an author. I can only hope that it brought enjoyment to you, the reader, as well. And, of course, that you will come back for the remaining books in the Men of the Ice series to see what your favorite Generals players are up to, and who might be next in the lineup to demand his own story. These guys—and their girls—love to surprise me.

As always, I am grateful to everyone who has helped me along the way in my publishing journey. Your support and encouragement means the world.

This series would definitely not be where it is today without the help of my personal assistant, Valentina Rodriguez, in the promotion of branding of the series. She's the reason that Char's Foundation's charity cookbook is a real thing. Yes, it is—and if you want an electronic copy, just find me on social media (the best place is my Facebook group) and request it.

Michele Shriver writes women's fiction and contemporary romance. Her books feature flawed-but-likeable characters in real-life settings. She's not afraid to break the rules, but never stops believing in happily ever after. Michele counts among her favorite things a good glass of wine, a hockey game, and a sweet and sexy book boyfriend, not necessarily in that order.

Contact:

Website: www.micheleshriver.com
Twitter: www.twitter.com/micheleshriver
Facebook:
https://www.facebook.com/AuthorMicheleShriver
Email: micheleshriver@gmail.com

For contests, special gifts, advance reader copies of my books and the chance to hang out and chat and keep up to date on all my publishing news, please consider joining my Facebook group:
https://www.facebook.com/groups/721292531291721/

For more about the Generals and the Men of the Series, visit the website and Facebook page:

Website: https://menoftheice.wordpress.com/
Facebook: https://www.facebook.com/MenoftheIce

CPSIA information can be obtained
at www.ICGtesting.com
Printed in the USA
LVOW12s0019260517

535899LV00003B/220/P

9 781537 740867